Death
by
Detention

To Sophia

Sparkly wishes!

Ali Sparkes

Designed by Thomas Miller Creative Ltd.
www.thomasmillerltd.com

Illustrations by Scott Lancaster-Collier
www.justjolt.co.uk

TEEN OPS

Death
by
Detention

BY
ALi SPARKES

Detained

PLEASE READ THIS THROUGH CAREFULLY BEFORE YOU BEGIN.

'Yeah, *right*,' muttered Elliot.

'Elliot – the sign says SILENCE. And that's what it means.'

Elliot gritted his teeth. It was taking all his self-control not to screw up the exam paper and throw it right in Mr Gallagher's face. In fact, if Gallagher wasn't built like a heavyweight boxer, he probably would.

Something wet hit his ear as soon as Gallagher turned away. He looked down at his elbow where the missile had landed. It slid onto the desk in a trail of drooly bubbles. A chewed up bit of pink bubble-gum, still with Shania's teeth marks embedded in it. He turned to give her a murderous look. He'd hit a lot of people, but never a girl before. Shania wasn't a normal girl, though, was she? Maybe he'd make an exception.

Shania was sniggering at him while she pretended to read the exam paper. As if. She might be tougher than half the boys in Year 11, but everyone knew she had the brain of a Tellytubby. On a slow day. The only thing she ever read was HEAT magazine. And then she moved her lips. He wondered why Gallagher bothered. Here they were, at 5pm, hours after school had shut, taking some meaningless exam when they could all be doing something else. Gallagher must know that there wasn't a hope of either of them achieving anything above a big fat zero. What was the point?

A raucous punk song suddenly burst through the air. Shania plucked her phone out of her pocket and peered at it with interest. Gallagher was across the room like lightning.

'Don't even think about it, Shania,' he growled as she went to press ACCEPT CALL. He knocked the mobile out of her hand and into his own and detached its battery before shoving the two parts into his jacket pocket. Then he went back to sitting on the wide, high windowsill of the classroom, his feet resting on the back of a chair. He stared down at them both for a few seconds before he spoke.

'You may think you're here as a punishment,' he said. 'But you're not. You're here because I happen to believe that you're not a pair of brain-dead thugs.'

That stopped Shania, mid-chew. Her eyes, startlingly blue beyond all the black and red eyeliner, widened, and an impressed kind of smirk wove across her narrow face. She tugged at her elaborately spiked

2

blonde hair and waited for Gallagher to go on, as if he was about to deliver the punchline to a joke.

Which he kind of was, thought Elliot. This whole set up was a joke. He was a *thug*. And he might as well be brain dead. Shania too. They were both a waste of space in this school and everyone in this room knew it.

'I believe-' went on Gallagher, but he never got to finish that sentence.

The window smashed and blood exploded from Gallagher's head.

Red drops and diamonds of shattered glass fell across Elliot's exam paper like rain.

Their head teacher had been shot.

Grey Matter

Elliot had seen plenty of exploding heads. Shedloads of them. Heads exploded all the time on Death Duty and Zombie Stalkers IV. Mr Gallagher's end was not so spectacular - there was a fine spray of blood and some pale grey stuff which might have been parts of his brain; it was hard to tell. Elliot was crouching under the table and couldn't see properly. The head teacher's body had slewed sideways onto the classroom floor in a shower of broken glass. His left arm and shoulder was all Elliot could see. It was motionless.

'Omigodomigodomigod.' Shania was under the next table along, doing a shrieky kind of whisper. Elliot stared at her until she raised her eyes from the collapsed head teacher and peered across at him. Beneath all the make-up and attitude she looked about six years old. 'He's dead!' she whispered. 'Dead! Isn't he..?'

Elliot wanted to crawl across and find out the truth - even though he knew it would not be pretty. But something made him stop.

He urgently put his finger to his lips and shook his head. The sudden crash of the shattering window and the shock of what had just happened had left a kind of audible fog in his ears for a few seconds - but now it abruptly lifted and Elliot could hear something else above his and Shania's panicky breathing.

Footsteps. Crunching on gravel.

Whoever had shot Gallagher was outside. And maybe they weren't finished yet.

Elliot began to crawl rapidly across the scuffed vinyl tiles of the classroom floor. He gestured at Shania to do the same. To his surprise she didn't make any fuss - she just followed him, squirming along in his wake as low down as she could get.

Elliot's heart and lungs were pumping oxygen through him like two frenzied engines. The whumping and wheezing seemed to fill the entire room, although he knew it was mostly inside his panicked head. The classroom door was ajar and just three seconds' crawl away - but what if the sniper outside was watching? Aiming? Just taking his sweet time before picking them both off?

Or what if he hadn't seen them at all yet - but the movement of the door as they crawled around it alerted him? Beyond it, the red polished tiles of the main corridor looked like a river of blood. Elliot knew his shocked mind was playing tricks - making him think that. He'd never ever thought that before. That corridor was just the corridor - and now their best hope of not getting shot. That was the truth.

'Come on! Come ooooon!' whimpered Shania, bumping into him from behind. He could hear the hysteria mounting in her voice. She might start screaming at any second. He nudged the door and it eased open with a gentle gliding arc. There was no hiding the movement. He slithered around it and got to his feet on the other side of the corridor wall. As soon as Shania had done the same they just stood there, staring at each other in bewildered disbelief.

'What-?' began Shania but then there was a thud and a crunch following by the unmistakable sound of a glass pane being shoved inward.

Without a word they tore off down the corridor, terror shooting hot bursts of adrenalin through their muscles.

They made no plan. Neither of them discussed it. But they made straight for reception - the only way out, with a student ID card swipe, at this time of day. 'Why - why did someone shoot Mr Gallagher?' gasped Shania as their feet slapped too noisily along the tiles and their gasps blatted back off the painted brick walls. 'What's going on?!'

'How should I know?' Elliot puffed back. 'I'm not planning to ask them, are you?!'

'No,' said Shania. Which was possibly the most sensible response he'd ever got from her since they'd met in Year 4.

Reception was moments away when Elliot remembered his ID card was back in his bag. And then he realized they couldn't go on anyway. At first he had no idea why he knew this - but he was totally certain. He suddenly halted, grabbing at Shania's arm and shoving her to the floor. She gave a furious grunt but - with more sense of self-preservation than he'd ever have given her credit for - she then shut herself up, rolled against the corridor wall and lay still.

Elliot did the same. Why? There was nobody in the reception area - he could tell. The high curved desk where the secretaries sat was empty; the school office staff having left half an hour or more ago. So what was different? Then he realized. It was the light. It was winter and already nearly fully dark outside and the school kept lights on for security around the school's access points. But not now. Reception was dark. Except for a tiny beam of red - like a phantom needle pricking through the gloom. The beam spun and angled erratically and then settled. Steadied itself.

'It's a laser sight,' he hissed, barely able to believe he was even saying it out loud. It was preposterous! That was not a word that often passed through his mind (his English teacher would have been overjoyed) but it was the best fit. He wasn't at home, playing Clan of the Assassin or Urban Soldier. He was in school! On a Wednesday evening in late November. In detention, like he'd been so many times before.

'No,' said Shania, suddenly, as if she'd decided. 'This isn't real.'

It was exactly what he'd been thinking. His brain kept flipping and shrugging, trying to throw off this insane situation it was being presented with. But still the laser beam hovered in reception. At head height. And then he realised something with horrible clarity. It wasn't just hanging there in the air randomly. It was waiting for a target.

F.A.B.

'We can't get out through there,' whispered Elliot. 'Someone's waiting. They've got a gun. I can see the laser sight.'

'Gym,' said Shania.

It was what he'd been thinking too. At the far end of the gym was a double door - an exit onto the school fields during the day and an emergency exit at other times. Elliot crawled back along the corridor and Shania followed him. The gym was down the far end. The corridor ran the length of one side of the building, with windows at waist height, giving onto a quadrangle courtyard where the kids would go and hang out, eat lunch on wooden benches and torment the goldfish in the square concrete pond. The pond was meant to offer an oasis of calm in the frenetic world of GCSEs and SATs. It was a nice idea; a kind of Secondary School Feng Shui experiment. It had been officially opened by the mayor, a plump red-haired woman who had told them that a water feature was good for the school's energy patterns or 'chi'. Two weeks later the caretaker had to put a metal grid over it to stop kids like Elliot dropping other kids into it. Apparently having a whimpering Year 7 splashing frenziedly in one corner played havoc with the 'chi'. And the ceaseless rain of Wotsits poisoned most of the fish.

As they scrabbled along on hands and knees, Elliot risked bobbing up to take a glance across the quad. It was in darkness but a low moon gleamed across the mosaic of pond water and in it he saw a shadow flitting from left to right. It was man-sized. In the millisecond his brain took to make out the shape and the movement, Elliot worked out that the figure had turned towards him just as he'd ducked down again.

He let out a curse. 'What?' Shania hissed.

'There's someone out there,' he hissed back, slamming himself against the wall, beneath the window. Shania did the same. They pressed themselves as tightly against the old fibreboard panels as they could. 'Don't move,' breathed Elliot. Deep in shadow, it would be hard for anyone on the other side of the glass to look down and see what was at the foot of the wall on the inside. Shania was skinny and no part of her was in the shaft of moonlight that painted half of the corridor floor. He, too, was inside the gloom. Elliot's chest and left cheek was flush against the panel. He raised his eyes to the glass and waited.

Nothing. For several seconds. And then... just as he was about to get up and move on... a click and a sudden bloom of opaque mist across the window, a metre above him. A dark face pressed against it. Seemed almost to press through it. He heard a whimper escape his throat. He was so scared he thought he might actually wet himself. But then the face and the breath mist vanished and he heard the definite crunch of footsteps on gravel - retreating.

A colourful stream of curses hissed out like escaping steam. 'I nearly peed my pants,' concluded a voice somewhere near his feet. He had forgotten about Shania, in the midst of his terror. Now she got to her feet and ran, stooped low, to the end of the corridor. Her shadow loomed and flickered as she went and as he moved to go after her, he paused, suddenly realizing that maybe he should run in the opposite direction. If she got seen, the gunman would chase after her and he would have a better chance of escape. Probably better all round if she screwed up like she always did and crashed into something. Shania's famous stupidity might be his best hope of saving his own skin.

And yet he followed her. The gym was still the only escape route he could think of right now. The large hall was in darkness when he caught up with her. She was pressing down hard on the double bars of the exit doors. 'They won't open!' she wailed. 'They're stuck!'

He ran across to shove at the bars, which lay horizontally at waist height and just below a sign reading 'THIS DOOR IS ALARMED'. It's not the only one, thought Elliot. And then another thought occurred. What if they triggered the alarm? The gunman or gunmen would be alerted that someone else was in the building. Up until this point, they might believe that the headteacher they'd just shot was alone. If an alarm went off it would be clear somebody else was in the building.

But as the doors wouldn't shift in the slightest, this wasn't something they needed to worry about. Shania abruptly turned away from them. With a squeak of her Doc Martens, she went up the climbing bars on the wall. She peered down through the high gym windows and swore with feeling. 'They've driven a truck right up against the doors!' she reported, sounding amazed. 'Some black four-by-four with this metal thing at the front like - you know - like a bloody Thunderbirds thing. Rammed up against the doors!'

Elliot felt a chill run through him. Whoever had shot Mr Gallagher wasn't some loner with a grudge, wandering past and taking a pot shot. They had blocked off all obvious exits. This was *organised*.

'What the hell do they want?' he murmured.

Shania shrugged, hanging from the bars like a punk monkey. 'To kill the head teacher,' she said. 'I wanted to kill him about ten minutes ago. But not - you know - actually. Wow. I can't believe he's really dead.'

'Can we get out of the windows?' asked Elliot.

They looked around at the tall glass panels on three sides of the building. It was an old fashioned school, built in the 1960s. The windows were sealed units apart from some about four metres up which could be tilted open by the caretaker with a hook on a very long pole. The pole in question was clipped into an upright position in one corner of the gym. They could get it and use it easily enough. In fact Elliot already had. Last term, he and Mitchell Lewin had re-enacted a jousting scene from history, using the vaulting horse and the window hook pole. Mitchell lost a tooth and Elliot ended up with mild concussion. And an exclusion warning. Even if they opened the windows and climbed up to them, there was a stupid, skull-smashing drop on the other side.

'No good here,' said Elliot. 'The windows that open are in the classrooms. Or the dining hall. Let's go.'

'Wait,' hissed Shania, still up on the bars. 'I can see one.'

As she spoke a thin blue beam of light swept the ceiling. She shrank back against the bars, which were closely fixed to the walls. Elliot froze as torchlight cut through the gloom within centimetres of Shania's face. Then it dropped again, severed by the window sill. And he could hear voices.

'There's more than one,' whispered Shania. 'Come on - get up here. You can look in the other direction. We need to know how many we're up against.'

He nodded and climbed swiftly up the bars to her right. High up, he could easily see outside. Scanning across the concrete area behind the gym, he saw two men walking towards the black 4x4. They were dressed in dark clothing and balaclavas and carrying guns. They looked as if they'd stepped right out of Death Duty IV. Again, Elliot struggled to make his mind accept that this was real. His brain kept checking. And re-checking. Surely this was virtual reality? Surely he was really just in bed in his room at home, wireless controller in hand, in the early hours, tired and drunk with gameplay but too wired to let it go and sleep? Any second now, Dave would come in and pull the plug, belt him round the head and yell at him.

'Stop breathing so loud!' grunted Shania. 'Shut up and listen!'

But the voices down below were muffled and indistinct. The men walked around the 4x4 and then got into it. Dipped sidelights came on at the front, adding the faintest yellow glow to the moonlit wall and doors.

Elliot's heart leapt with hope. 'They're going!' he whispered.
Shania said nothing.

The 4x4 engine started up. It had a quiet, steady engine; the engine of a very expensive car. The 4x4 backed away from the double doors and a metallic creak could be heard inside the gym as the brace against the doors fell away.

'They're going!' repeated Elliot.

Still Shania said nothing. She watched the scene below with a face like wax. He'd seen the look before. Usually when a teacher was having a go at her. No emotion. Just a bored mask.

The car stopped and the long, rectangular metal brace thing on its bumper retracted with a sudden flip and a smooth glide, into a space beneath the grille. The grille then slid down over it. Shania was right. It *was* like something out of Thunderbirds. Then the engine noise subsided and the vehicle's lights went off. The two men got out and walked back to the double doors. And opened them.

Inconvenience

Shania hooked her right arm right through the bars and clenched her left hand around her right wrist in a grip so tight that later she'd see finger shaped bruises. She was trembling so hard she felt sure the whole rack of climbing bars would start to rattle like a freight train at any second. Elliot, beside her, had also frozen as the men shoved open the double doors and walked into the darkened gym.

'I told you,' said one of them. 'He's the only one here. All the staff went home half an hour ago. I watched them all out. I know what I'm doing.'

'If you knew what you were doing, you'd have made a cleaner shot of it, wouldn't you? But you left a mess'. The second man sounded older than the first, and his voice was full of contempt. His accent was neutral. He could have been from anywhere in the south of the country.

The younger sounding one definitely had a slight Cockney twang. A bloody fox shot out of the hedge, just as I went for it,' he retorted.' 'And it only threw me off a millimetre. I still hit the target.'

'You checked? Close up?'

'I didn't need to. His brains are all over the floor.'

'We'll bring the body out this way,' said Man 2. 'The grounds back here have much better cover. And I want to be sure there's nobody else in the building. No witnesses.'

'I told you – there's nobody,' snapped Man 1. 'I did my research. No after school clubs on tonight – all the staff clocked out and gone. No cleaners due in until 6am. No caretaker on sight. Gallagher doing his final rounds on his own, as usual. And the alarm and the phones are all knocked out. I'm not a bloody amateur!'

'So you keep telling me,' said Man 2. There was a harsh crackle before Man 1 could respond and Man 2 whipped a two-way radio from his belt.

Trembling four metres above, Shania saw a tiny dot of green light on the radio as Man 2 held it up. A curt, compressed voice came from the gadget. 'Cain – Abel. All clear at your end? Ready to sweep?'

'Affirmative, David,' said Man 2. 'We're in the gym and proceeding to point of contact. We'll search as we go. Cain will go in tandem with me and Goliath can bar the exit behind us.'

'Affirmative,' said the voice on the radio – this 'David'. 'Goliath, move in now.' Immediately the soft rumble of the 4x4 engine started up and ten seconds later the gym doors juddered.

Glancing along the high windows to her left, Shania saw the vehicle's wide metal shovel was clamped against the outside of the doors again. So... there were at least four men here – two outside the school; one of them driving the car. Their best hope of slipping out as soon as the men below had moved on had gone up in smoke. They would have to find an exit deeper inside the school.

'Be ready for my signal, Goliath,' said Cain. 'David – we're sweeping now. See you at the contact point in five. Stay in touch.'

The radio crackled another affirmative and both men set off, pausing only to swipe open the games store cupboard. They found the light switch, spilling a golden shaft across the gloomy gym. Shania's bladder threatened to burst with fear. What if the light picked them out? She cursed herself for wearing shiny patent leather Doc Martens.

But the men did not look up. They looked around the cupboard, poking quickly through its contents before agreeing that the store was empty of human life. Then they gave the large square gym a cursory glance. Still, they did not look up.

Five seconds later, the gym doors were swinging shut behind them. Elliot moved down a rung. 'STOP!' she hissed. 'Not YET! WAIT!'

'Who made you boss?' he grunted back, but he did stop. They waited for perhaps two minutes before Shania realised there would be a localised shower if she stayed up here any longer. If she didn't get to the toilet soon she would be peeing her pants in front of a boy. There was no good way of looking at that.

Elliot decided he didn't need to take orders from Shania. After a short wait he began to climb down the bars. It was tough work because his limbs had totally seized up while the men were in the gym. To stop himself collapsing from sheer panic he had just become stone; a rock-like limpet grown from the metal rungs. But now they'd gone the fight or flight instinct had kicked back in big time and his heart was like something trapped in his ribcage, trying to jackhammer its way out.

As he began to climb down, shaking and sweating, Shania informed him that she needed to urinate, urgently. She didn't put it that way. Her version contained more Fs and Ps than this but you couldn't ever accuse her of not getting to the point.

'So go then!' he'd replied.

'I will. But you're coming in with me,' she stated. It wasn't a request.

'I'm not going in the girls' toilets!'

'YES YOU ARE!' she growled as she reached the floor. 'We stick together! It's probably our only chance of getting out of here alive.'

Elliot didn't agree. He felt he'd stand a much better chance on his own. But the toilets were right outside the gym doors and he needed to go too. Fight or flight. In nature this often meant evacuating bladder, bowels and stomach - sometimes all at once - to create a lighter load and better odds for the prey to run for its life. He guessed he should be grateful that he only needed to pee.

They moved quietly across the gym floor and eased the doors to the corridor open gently. No torch light flashed in the short stretch of corridor ahead of them so they stepped out of the gym. Elliot made to go right, into the boys' toilets and changing rooms but Shania grabbed his left elbow before he could even take a step.

'Oh no!' she said. 'You STAY with me!'

'What am I? Your dog?!' he bit back, but he didn't fight as she dragged him into the girls' toilets to the left.

She sprinted into a cubical and closed the door fast – but quietly. The velocity of water he heard next would not have shamed a bull rhino. He hurried into the cubicle at the far end to unleash his own pressure jet. He didn't think he'd ever been so relieved to let his bladder go.

For a moment or two afterwards there was a strained silence in the darkened room. The wall over the cistern was scrawled with graffiti in the girls' toilets too, Elliot noted, with mild surprise. He could just make it out from the outside light which crept through the frosted glass window to his left. Apparently Lucy Shayer was a slapper.

What – the one who played oboe and had won a Duke of Edinburgh Award medal? Who knew? None of the boys did, for sure.

A voice floated quietly across the four cubicles between them. 'Don't flush,' it advised. 'They might hear us.'

Elliot stepped back out. Shania followed and automatically washed her hands under a silent dribble of tap water. 'How are we going to get out of here?' she asked and for the first time since Gallagher had been shot he heard her voice shake. It was a weird thing to hear. Shania Laker was all hard-glazed attitude - 24/7. He had never seen a single crack in her shell until today.

Elliot took a long breath. 'We need to reach the classrooms and get out of a window,' he said. The gym building was out on a spur with a single corridor leading to it. The classrooms were along the long walkway which led off, right and left, at the end of this corridor. At this moment, their part of the building seemed to have been 'swept' by Gallagher's killers, but they would be coming back, wouldn't they? That guy had said they'd bring the body back through the gym. There was no telling how far around the school they had now swept and at what moment they would retrace their steps.

'So – how do we know we won't smack right into them?' asked Shania.

'We don't,' said Elliot. Even in the gloom he saw her roll her eyes. 'Well – have you got a better idea?!'

'It's this stupid school's fault!' she snapped.

'What – that masked gunmen are stalking us through the corridors?!'

'That we can't get help! If they didn't take our phones every day we'd have them right here and could call the police, couldn't we?'

He shrugged. 'That's what schools do. They take your phone.' Mobiles were banned in school, but – because some parents complained when they couldn't call their kids seconds after school ended - Mr Gallagher had allowed phones to be brought in and handed in to reception each day. The receptionists, with quite enough to do without running a mobile phone check in service, had complained - and now a different teacher had to take a turn each day, collecting the phones and putting them in plastic zip-up bags with the student's ID number written across them in marker pen. As lessons began, the phone cupboard was locked and then the key-holding teacher had to come back at the end of the day to hand out all the phones again.

It was stupid and annoying. But Elliot could see why they did it. It was hard enough to get teenagers to concentrate in Physics without Pokemon going on under half the tables. Of course, it was easy enough to smuggle a phone in – nobody was getting searched – but if they were caught their phone would be confiscated for a week. And if they were caught again – for a month.

'It's against our rights!' declared Shania. 'They've just got NO respect!'

Elliot snorted. 'Yeah. Well, it's a two way thing, isn't it? And anyway, you just ignore them and sneak it in all the time. And then you're too dumb to put your phone on silent. If you had half a brain cell you wouldn't have had to hand your phone over to Gallagher just before he got shot and we could have phoned for help ages ago.'

'It was after school,' she began, and then her eyes widened. 'Wait! My phone is still in his pocket!' she gasped.

'You want to go back and get it?'

She folded her arms and slumped against the basins. 'Alright – so – what are we going to do?'

'We could just wait here,' said Elliot. He was still sweating with fear but the extreme panic had now left him and his heart was just racing rather than doing an Olympic sprint. 'They'll come back this way with... with Gallagher... but they probably won't look in here again.'

She shook her head. 'I can't believe he's dead. Why? Why the hell would anyone want to shoot a teacher?'

He snorted. 'You're asking *me*?' Last term he had been excluded for two weeks after smashing the headlights on Mr Ratner's car.

'Don't be stupid!' she said. 'You're just an angry puppy because your Dad pushed off. Everyone knows that's why you act up. You're not so tough, Hickman.'

'What the hell do *you* know about it?!' Elliot felt instant rage pulsing through his fear.

'Well – dur!' she said, pulling an idiot face. 'We've been in the same year since primary! I haven't forgotten what a good little boy you were in Year 5, you know. Then your dad walks out and – oh no – poor baby Elliot gets all kicky and thumpy and stops reading books!'

Elliot felt his mouth drop open. He was furious – but also staggered at her assessment of his recent life. In two sentences she'd summed him up and made him sound like the lamest loser on the planet.

'You think you know it all, don't you?' was all he managed to say.

'Yeah, well, it don't take a psychiatrist,' she said, turning away from him and going to peer through the frosted glass window in the far wall.

'You don't know anything!' he muttered. It wasn't just Dad leaving. It was all the stuff that came afterwards. The stuff called Dave.

She was in silhouette by the window and staring up at the top panel. 'I reckon I could get through that,' she said.

The window opened, true, but the opening part was just a shallow oblong of glass which tilted out at the top. Elliot weighed up Shania's frame. She was skinny - but not that skinny.

'You won't fit through there,' he said.

She spun around at once. 'Are you saying I'm fat?!'

'Fat? No. You're a stick insect. But you've still got an arse and that won't fit through there.'

'Are you saying my arse is fat?'

Elliot sighed. He should never have got into this. Then he reminded himself that he really didn't care. 'Yeah,' he said. 'You've got an arse the size of Jupiter. It blots out the sun.'

That did it. Shania immediately scrambled up onto the window sill and reached for the top window. It opened with an alarmingly loud grating noise and both of them sucked in their breath. For a few seconds, Shania remained still, listening - but when no sudden shouts or hurried steps - or bullets - followed, she began to worm her way through the window.

'You won't get through!' hissed Elliot. 'Don't be stupid!'

'Watch and learn!' she grunted back, her legs kicking out behind her now as she wriggled her upper body across the thin metal frame.

Elliot gritted his teeth. 'Even if you get through - I won't!'

'So?' she called back. And then, after a pause, she added: 'I'll go for help, dummy!'

But he wasn't so sure because now that she'd got as far out as her waist, her hands gripping the outside of the window frame and her whole body teetering like a see-saw, he could see that her lower half wasn't easily going to follow. And Shania finally seemed to be getting the message now, as a torrent of hushed curses rained down the far side of the glass.

'What was it you said?' asked Elliot. 'Watch and learn?'

She threw back some particularly colourful words and then went suddenly rigid. Elliot froze too. He didn't need to ask what the problem was. A beam of blue torchlight had suddenly bisected the dim greyness outside.

Shania was trapped in the window frame and the killers were coming.

Suspended

Elliot had never in his entire life imagined he would get up close and personal with Shania Laker. They might both be side by side in the 'troubled student' file but he had never wanted anything to do with her. All her posturing and stupid hair and heavy eye make-up was such a cliché. But then, isn't that just what she thought about him? he wondered, briefly, as he grabbed her legs and began tugging her back through the window. It must have hurt but there was no time to be gentle. The torchlight had continued to wave around in the darkness but had not yet fallen directly upon the girls' toilet window. There was just a chance she could get back in before she was seen.

He heard her give out only a tiny whimper as he hauled her back over the metal ledge. Her school shirt and jumper had ridden up on the return journey and her bare skin must have been scraped horribly. Three seconds later she thumped back to the floor and Elliot shoved her down onto the grubby tiles - a moment before the torchlight flooded across the frosted glass above them.

For maybe ten seconds it waved around and then they heard the crackling cough of another two way radio and then a low voice just outside the window. 'Abel - come in.'

A crackle and then: 'What's up, Goliath?'

'Did you check the toilets by the gym?'

'Affirmative.'

'Well, check again. I think I just saw something.'

Elliot and Shania shuddered with fright.

'Cain is on the way,' said Abel. 'Stay where you are and watch the exits, Goliath. And send Jonah in. We need back up.'

'Affirmative.' The torchlight suddenly formed a clear halo on the window, as if the man outside was trying to see through the obscured glass.

'Any movement outside, Goliath?'

'Negative. The perimeter trips have been set up. Nothing's gone off. Nobody but us will be leaving alive.'

'Oh my god!' whispered Shania and Elliot thought she might be crying. He didn't blame her. He thought he might be crying too. He had never been so afraid in his life as that pale beam shafted around the room, lighting up the cubicle doors, the grimy basins and the damp-blotched ceiling tiles. How were they going to get out of this? Was he fated to spend the last few minutes of his pathetic life, shivering, whimpering and staring at the stained ceiling of the girls' toilets at Oakwood Academy? With a girl he had never liked?

'Wait!' he whispered, as the light pulled back and the man outside stepped away, presumably to patrol the exits, as ordered. 'The ceiling! It's a false one, isn't it?'

'So?' gulped Shania.

'There's - like - a maintenance grid up above it - so you can get up there and work on the electrics or the plumbing.' He remembered a tile punching up and dropping out of the frame when he and Aaron Miller had been chucking Sebastian Brownlow's shoes around the boys' changing room a while back. 'I've seen it,' he said. 'The ceiling tiles just push up and you can get up there.'

Shania didn't waste a moment - she was into the nearest cubicle and up on the cistern within seconds. Elliot followed her, just in time to catch the ceiling tile she had punched through its frame before it crashed onto the toilet and confirmed the suspicions of the guy outside. 'Careful!' he hissed. She was looking into the void above. The ceiling tiles were large - paving slab size - and she was already reaching through to find the metal grid above which the caretaker could climb up into for maintenance and repairs.

'Let me go first,' he murmured.

'Why?!'

'Because I'm taller than you and I'm strong enough to pull you up after me,' he pointed out. She didn't argue but stepped down onto the closed toilet lid, and let him up first. Elliot had never imagined that his PE lessons would one day pay off. PE and games were the only thing he ever put much effort into these days - mostly because it seemed to help with the endless, seething pit of anger which lived in his belly. It was a tough, macho thing to do chest presses and pull ups on the bar, supporting your own weight. All the sporty boys tried to outdo each other. Mr Rayner had once said he had a chance at competing at county level if he pursued gymnastics. But that was before he'd had his car lights smashed. Mr Rayner bothered with Elliot Hickman a lot less these days.

Now, though, it was pay off time. Elliot grasped the strong metal bars and easily hauled himself up onto the grid above the suspended ceiling. There was only about a metre of headroom but it was enough. He wormed backwards along the grid, which was like a horizontal ladder, and then reached down to haul Shania up too, anchoring his feet under a metal rung. 'Wait – pass me the ceiling tile!' he remembered, right at the last moment. She did, passing it up through the gap at an angle. He put it safely aside and then hoisted her up, trying not to grunt with the effort. She couldn't have weighed more than 90lbs but pulling her up at such a tight angle was killing his arms, shoulders and abs. As soon as she was up on the grid, hunched over like a squirrel, he breathed out and dropped the ceiling tile back into the frame from above. It settled back in without complaint. A heartbeat later the girls' toilet door crashed open.

Health & Safety

Shania finally understood what the term 'cold sweat' really meant. Beads of moisture had prickled across her shoulders, arms and back as she lay on the toilet floor after so nearly getting caught in that window. She could see her own limp body, hanging down from the window like rabbit in a butcher's shop, having been shot neatly between the eyes.

She knew that without Elliot dragging her back in, she would be dead. She supposed she ought to thank him but there was no time to do anything but breathe and sweat. And now she was crouched in a ceiling space, her temperature dropping so fast she imagined the sweat was turning to ice on her skin. She was probably in shock. But at least she wasn't gasping or gulping for air. In fact, she didn't think she was breathing at all. She and Elliot were silent and still as statues as the man called Cain crashed into the room below. He whacked open the doors of each of the six cubicles, one by one and then informed his team that there was nothing there. 'You done wasting my time, Goliath?!' he snapped. 'We've got bigger problems.'

And then he was gone again. Shania heard him ranting in his slight cockney twang - either into the radio or to himself, she wasn't sure - as he headed back up the corridor. She couldn't make out what he said apart from the word 'resurrection'. Maybe this whole Biblical names thing they had going meant they were part of some barmy religious cult. Maybe they disapproved of the way Gallagher had been running school assembly.

Suddenly there was a click and a dim light spread around her. Elliot's face, close by, was a mask of fear, but he was pointing to a dusty panel on the wall with a series of switches on it. 'Maintenance guy lighting!' he whispered. 'And look-' he pointed around them. 'No walls!'

She realised what he meant at once. The lay out of the walls below was not carried on up here. There were many struts and supporting brick columns - but no walls. They could see out across a vast area of dimly lit roof space, filled with ducting, wiring and metal boxes. It was dusty, draped in cobwebs and probably home to myriads of spiders and rats – but it didn't seem to contain any masked assassins, which was definitely a plus.

'So we can move across here,' went on Elliot in a voice just above a whisper. 'We can get across to the ceilings above the classrooms – get down and get out of a window.'

She nodded. 'But how will we know where we are? We can't see through the ceiling!'

'We'll just have to try to work it out and then lift a ceiling tile when we think we're in the right place.'

'And what if there's a sniper underneath us?!'

'You got a better idea?'

She shook her head. No. She hadn't.

'Go carefully – climb across the metal,' he said, shuffling around and pointing his head in what looked like the direction of the classrooms. 'For god's sake don't put your knee or your hand on the ceiling tiles. They'll just break!'

'I had worked that out!' she hissed.

'Go slowly. We don't know how much noise we're making,' he added.

She just made a rude gesture at his backside as it shuffled ahead of her. It wasn't that everything he was saying wasn't perfectly sensible – it's just the way he assumed she hadn't worked any of it out for herself. But that's what people always did with her. Just because she didn't care about getting grades, people assumed she was stupid. As far as she was concerned, she was going to be the lead singer in an all-girl punk band and honestly – you didn't need ten GCSEs for that. Or for the job in ASDA she'd have to endure while she was still working on the fame and money side of the band.

Tania, the senior house parent at the home, was always wittering on about a 'fall back career' but she totally missed the point. Planning for a 'fall back career' was admitting defeat before you even started. Her ambition was pure. Her passion was total. Studying for stupid exams which were going to mean nothing to her five minutes after she turned 16, was just a pointless distraction. A betrayal, even.

She had realised, a while back, that it was actually better to pretend to be thick because then you avoided those kinds of teachers who felt they could change your life for you. They particularly loved it if they could change the life of a kid in care. You could see it in their earnest little faces – *I can help you! I will guide and inspire you and you will get GCSEs with prospects rather than pregnant with piercings!* Well, she wasn't likely to get GCSEs and she was absolutely *never* getting pregnant, so they really needn't bother. She was undecided about the piercings.

Elliot suddenly stopped dead and she nearly head-butted his bum. She didn't say anything. She waited, listening.

There was movement below them. Where? Were they over a classroom? A corridor? The school kitchen? Now she heard voices and once again recognized the man calling himself Cain. '...just five minutes ago! ...no! No way. He's dead, no question. Someone's messing with us.'

The voice on the two-way radio sounded just as agitated. 'I'm coming in. You sweep this floor from west to east, Jonah is going east to west. I'll sweep upstairs from the west – Abel is working across from the east. Goliath will have to take the perimeter alone.' 'I can manage this level, David,' said Cain, sounding resentful. 'Keep Jonah outside. We need eyes on the exits!'

'If you had *managed* from the start, we'd be out clean by now,' spat back David, who seemed to be the boss of this outfit. 'Sweep every room and cupboard. If anything moves – shoot it.'

Shania shuddered. Elliot turned slowly to exchange a look with her. It was small comfort to see that he was as terrified as she was. Below them, Cain snapped: 'Affirmative. Out!' and then expelled a volley of abuse aimed, presumably, at David. *Someone's got issues with the management*, thought Shania.

Then her earring fell out.

It was a luminous green conical stud which poked defiantly out of her left earlobe. She wore it nearly all the time. It was a statement of who she was. Occasionally teachers tried to get her to take it out but she would say it was a religious symbol and they were persecuting her and generally make a huge fuss until they gave up. These days, they just ignored it. It was easier all round. It was only stupid health and safety nonsense after all.

As the earring fell onto the pale ceiling tile beneath the metal struts, the irony of Shania's little rebellion was brought home to her with cruel clarity. Her health and her safety were very much at issue right now. If her earring was a statement, right now it was stating that she was about to die.

Elliot's face was a mask of horror as the earring made a light 'tuk' noise before rolling in a little 'c' shape, back and forth along its conical plane with a gentle '*rrrrr ̲ rrrrr ̲ rrrrr*'.

If Cain had gone on cursing for five seconds longer he would not have heard, but he had lasped into silence just moments before the earring fell. And now they heard a low exhalation and a metallic click.

Then more silence followed. How many seconds or even minutes passed? Shania wasn't sure. It felt as if time had stopped. The tension was so thick it could have been a clear jelly which the three of them were suspended in. Everyone in the room - and above it - waited. Waited for someone to make the slightest noise.

The noise, when it came, wasn't slight. It was the sound of Elliot falling through the ceiling.

Resurrection

After all his good advice to Shania, Elliot had done his very best to keep to the metal struts and not place his weight between them where the ceiling tiles hung suspended in their flimsy framework. But in his terror he had frozen with his knee resting on a tile. Even so, it had held pretty well, thanks to a network of wiring feeding the lights to the classrooms and corridors below, which happened to angle across one half of the tile - but eventually it gave way and snapped. Elliot didn't even have time to scream as he dropped like a sack of sand.

And Cain had no time to scream, either, as a teenage boy struck him from above. The man was knocked back and hit the floor before Elliot did, partly breaking his fall. Elliot rolled and whacked his shoulder against a table, the air knocked out of him.

He scrambled to his feet as the gunman sprawled across the classroom floor, legs and arms flung out, like a dazed black spider.

His face was still masked and a gleaming black weapon - a SIG Sauer Pro semi-automatic if Elliot's Soldier Of Duty prowess was serving him properly - was still clutched in his gloved right hand. Through the broken ceiling dim light filtered down from the access space, lending a pale orange tinge to the strip of brow and cheekbone visible through the man's balaclava. Should he go for the SIG? Even as he thought this, the man's eyes suddenly sprang open and a second later he was up and the pistol was pointing directly at Elliot.

He did not speak to Elliot but pulled his radio out of its holster with his left hand, keyed it and spat out: 'All signs - I've found a hostile. It's a kid. He just fell out of the ceiling.'

There was a cacophony of response but Elliot heard only one word - 'eliminate'.

Before the elimination, though, Cain had a question or two. 'What are you doing here?'

'I - I was hiding,' croaked Elliot, holding his hands up weakly as if that might make any difference to his fate. He seemed to liquefy from his waist to his knees. He might be cacking his pants; he couldn't be sure. Images from his life began to tumble through his mind as if someone was emptying out a box of photos from the attic. He saw himself on a swing - felt Dad pushing him strongly with reassuring shouts. He was on stage, singing in a carol concert with his parents grinning at him from the audience. He was crying at his bedroom window and bashing on the glass as he saw Dad get in his old Peugeot and drive away. He was having a row with Dave and getting a slap.

'Why were you here after school?' The question cut coldly through the life-before-his-eyes montage.

'I was... in detention,' gulped Elliot. If these were his last words, it seemed bleakly fitting, somehow. His life had been detained. Permanently.

The man gave a dry laugh. 'Who with?'

'Mr Gallagher. He... he got shot,' rasped Elliot. 'I ran away.' At least, he thought, if it seemed like it was only him in detention, Shania might yet escape.

'So - you saw your head teacher die, did you?' asked Cain and his voice was soft - almost compassionate. But the gun did not for a second waver from its target. 'That's tough. And it's tough you had to be here, kid. Wrong time; wrong place.'

Elliot nodded, feebly.

'What did you do with the body?'

Elliot blinked. It was a question he hadn't expected. 'I - nothing - I - his brains were blown out. I couldn't help him. I crawled out of the room. And then I ran. Please don't kill me.'

'Sorry kid. It's nothing personal.'

The shot wasn't loud. The SIG was fitted with a silencer. But it still created a powerful thud as the bullet split the air, breaking the sound barrier. The thud as it impacted was barely more than a loud pop.

Elliot would have known nothing about it beyond the pop.

But as the bullet never hit him, he got a chance to hear and see everything. And he was screaming anyway, as if he had been hit. Because if real life had resembled Soldier Duty IV just seconds ago it had now abruptly shifted into a completely different game. WALKING APOCALYPSE III.

For Cain was suddenly on the floor, scrambling wildly to get up, his gun arm wrenched back behind him and his mouth covered by a blood-drenched hand. Looming over the gunman was the hunched figure of a man with his skull showing through a torn, flapping scalp.

Elliot screamed and fell backwards across the teacher's desk, scattering pens, books and unmarked essays in all directions. The dark figure raised its face to Elliot's and its eyes were blood red. Fluffy grey clumps of matter still stuck to the brown tweedy jacket as Cain's head was cracked brutally with the butt of his own gun. Some teachers act tough and others actually are. Even with his own brains spilling down his lapels, Mr Gallagher had resurrected himself.

Their headteacher was not dead.

He was undead.

Headspace

Shania scrambled across the struts as if the devil was chasing her. After what she'd heard below her there was every chance he was. As she'd listened to poor Elliot begging not to be killed she had thought she might be sick from pure fright. And that would be the end of her too. Some tiny thread of self-preservation had kept the heaving at bay, though, and then, with the gunshot and the screaming as cover, she had just followed instinct and scuttled away like a rat. She felt like a rat, too, leaving Elliot behind to whatever fate awaited him. She should have tried to help. If she had only been able to think of *how* to help, maybe she would have. Or maybe not. She was so scared. She had never known fear like this was even possible. It made her feel like a wild animal.

She crawled and crawled, whimpering and heedless of dust and spiders and roaming gunmen - until her head thwacked hard against a brick wall and she was forced to stop. She stared around her and realized that she had reached an outer wall of the school building. There was nowhere else to go. She couldn't keep going anyway - who knew how much noise her careless escape through the maintenance space had caused? She had to get down and find a window and get out.

Or maybe she didn't. Maybe she should just curl up in a ball here and wait for morning. These men could not stay forever. The school staff would be back first thing tomorrow. She peered at her watch, pressed its light and saw that it was now 6.17pm. She should have been home an hour ago. Would the home send someone to the school to look for her? She snorted. Of course not. She had a history of hanging out with mates in the town precinct until late evening – loudly practising her latest punk song offerings and scaring the late night shoppers. The home would assume she'd not bothered with tea and just gone straight there from her detention. Alarm bells wouldn't ring for a long time yet. Sometimes she got back around midnight. They tried to ground her but it didn't make much difference and with so many other harder nuts to crack at the home, she wasn't their big worry. She was actually pretty low maintenance.

So... the men searching the building had plenty of time to find her yet. What about Elliot though? He had a mum, didn't he? She might worry. Although it sounded like things weren't good at home. Cassie Burgess, in her tutor group, had said Elliot's mum had a boyfriend who'd been done for GBH. Looked like things were a bit tricky there so maybe Mrs Hickman wouldn't be expecting Elliot home soon either.

So. Sit tight and hope to live? Or try to get out?

42

Out. There was no way she was staying in here. School was bad enough when she was meant to be there, by law. This detention wasn't going on a moment longer than it had to.

Her eyes were much more accustomed to the light now. Small square lamps were affixed to the pillars dotted across this weird shallow loft. They couldn't be packing more than 15 watts - very weak, low energy bulbs - but she could clearly see a slant of darkness along the brick wall a few metres on from where she was crouched. As she peered at it hard she realised it was short flight of wooden steps, leading up beyond the headspace she was even now bumping against. How did that work? She was sandwiched between the ceiling to the ground floor and the wooden beams, boards and tiling of the floor above. There wasn't anywhere to go! And yet... there must be.

She listened for any movement below, in case one of the gunmen had followed the noise she'd made as she fled from Elliot's death scene. Nothing. And surely, if they had heard her, the ceiling would be peppered with bullets and she'd be a dead by now, her corpse hanging in the suspended ceiling and dripping blood onto the desks below like something out of a high school horror film. No. Amazingly, she had got away, unfollowed. Now she had to be extra careful and see if she could get away a bit more.

She crawled as silently as possible towards the wooden stairway and was on the first step seconds later, relieved to get her hands and knees off those godawful metal struts. There were seven or eight treads upwards and a little square well of headroom high enough to stand up in. At the top was a small, half height door. The maintenance access point – designed by a Hobbit. She would have to duck to get through it. She climbed up, wincing at every creak, and then tried the door. She shoved it hard, twisting on the metal ring set into it. It didn't shift. NO. Not locked. Not after all this! She twisted the metal ring the other way and shoved again.

She fell forward into a room.

And a second later a tall wild-haired figure was upon her.

Waterworks

Elliot staggered down the corridor, sucking air in through a throat which felt as if it had been crushed in a door. He was so shocked he could hardly remember how to walk. *No. No no no no no. Zombies were not real. Zombies were NOT REAL!*

But there was one in Mr Rathbone's geography class. And the only reason it wasn't eating his brains right now because it was busy eating the brains of Cain, the gunman. His head teacher was undead. A zombie! He had SEEN Gallagher shot with his own eyes. There was no way he could have mistaken the brain matter spattering out with the blood and broken glass. The man had been shot DEAD.

So how could he now be walking?

A distant flash of torchlight brought his hysterically chattering brain to silence and his frantic fleeing to a dead halt. There were multiple killers roaming the school. Whatever Gallagher was doing back in

Mr Rathbone's class, it wasn't important now. One gunman was down but at least four more were still on the hunt, three inside the building and one patrolling outside. And one was just around the bend of the corridor, flashing a blue beam around. He wondered why they hadn't just switched all the lights on, but then guessed that lighting up the whole school after hours might attract attention from people living nearby. Clearly this whole operation was meant to be about stealth. This was no terrorist publicity stunt.

The torch beam grew fatter and brighter. If he didn't move soon the gunman would be around the corner of the corridor and he'd be shot. Elliot dived through the open door to Mrs Garnet's Maths class. Keeping low he made for the windows on the far side. He scrabbled for the metal rod which levered the window shut, hooked across little pegs of iron. He lifted it as quietly as he could and then eased the window outward. There was plenty of space in the widening gap for him to slither through and sink into the waist deep foliage which hemmed the walls. But how much noise would he make? Just unhooking the window had seemed to create a metallic shriek worthy of an opera singer in a death scene.

Another flash in the corner of his eye decided the matter for him. He hauled himself up onto the sill and out through the window. The thud of his trainers and the crackle of leaves and twigs as he dropped into the hedging also crashed through his ears. He shrank down against the ground and let the leafy shrubs cover him. Maybe he'd done it. He was outside. In a few seconds he could run for it. If they were inside, searching, he could get away. Even if one was still outside, he couldn't be watching the entire school grounds at once, could he?

Elliot peered through a chink in the leaves to get his bearings and work out the best direction to run in. A moment later his heart gave a sickening thud. Beyond this hedge was a metre wide concrete path, another metre of scuffed grass and then a metal grid across a dark, shining rectangle. Elliot could have cried. Maybe he was crying. He was too appalled to notice. His mistake had been huge and was probably going to cost him his life.

He had exited through a classroom on the wrong side of the corridor. Mrs Garnet's room looked on to the quadrangle and its sorry excuse for a fish pond. There was no way out of here except back into the school.

The torchlight found him. 'Come on out, kid.'

Even if the man had been bluffing, Elliot's jolt of shock immediately gave him away. A dark figure was standing down the pathway next to one of the heavy wrought iron benches which were intended to support students as they gazed into the pool, thinking about Shakespeare. Or contemplating shrimpy, annoying kids struggling to get out of the weed and sludge.

The man raised his gun. Elliot reacted like an animal. He shot out of the shrubs and went directly over the pond, scrambling across the metal grid, while several goldfish made a panicky firework in the darkly reflected sky beneath.

The gunman did not give chase. What would be the point? His quarry had nowhere to run. It was a cat and mouse game. Elliot turned and saw the man grinning at him; his balaclava pulled up to reveal a broad white jaw and a set of gleaming teeth. Above them were two deep set dark eyes without a glimmer of mercy. He set down his torch on the concrete paving, letting it spread a thin light across the quad, while keeping his eyes and gun trained on Elliot all the while.

'You're a game one, I've got to give you that. Gave Cain the slip, did you? Well, I'm not so easy to avoid, kid.' He had a northern accent; Elliot guessed this must be Jonah – the guy sweeping east to west.

'Wait!' he whimpered, turning to face the man fully across the pond. He crouched down, instinctively making himself a smaller target. 'Just... why? Why is this happening?' He found himself tipping forward on the balls of his feet, nearly sprawling forward onto the pond cover. He locked his fingers into the cold metal grid, steadying himself as much as he could, rocking a little as it shifted slightly under him. It wasn't fixed down properly. That was a health safety issue, that was. He should raise that with his school council representative. Except that he was the one who'd unscrewed one end during a dull lunch break last week, while he'd pretended to look at the fish. He hadn't had time to do the other end.

Meanwhile, the man did wait. For what? A one line explanation? Would it help? It might send one unlucky kid on to the great hereafter feeling a bit less puzzled. But he'd still be dead.

'Your head teacher isn't quite what he seems, mate,' said the man, still grinning. 'He's a man with some very big enemies.'

Elliot's brain buzzed. Mr Gallagher? A man with enemies? It did not compute. Apart from the odd argument with the PTA or a bad news kid like him, Elliot simply couldn't imagine how a head teacher could get 'very big enemies'.

'Oh yeah,' said the gunman, nodding and still grinning at Elliot's obvious bafflement. 'You think he's just a teacher. Didn't you ever wonder why he looks like an Olympic athlete?'

'He - he used to teach sports,' burbled Elliot, still gripping the metal grid tightly. It shifted again; the far end lifting slightly and then dropping back down with a gritty thud.

'If you say so,' smirked the man. His gun remained level, steady and aimed. 'You have to be fit to be in special ops too.'

Elliot just gaped.

'And to kill people,' added the man. 'And to mess in business which he should leave alone. He shot my boss's big brother dead last year. And worse, he cost my boss a few million in profits and my boss doesn't like that kind of thing. So he sent us to sort out the problem. This time tomorrow your head teacher's body will be found floating in the Thames – and sending a very clear message to anyone else who wants to mess with our business.'

Elliot could think of no response. He was staggered. Mr Gallagher... some kind of British special agent? They guy had only been head for a few months but Elliot had never doubted his teacher background.

It was quite a revelation for his final moments.

'Too bad you had to get caught up in it,' the man added, before pulling the balaclava back down over his face. An odd thing to do, Elliot thought, bleakly, when there was no chance your victim would ever be able to identify you. Maybe the assassin felt just ashamed enough to want to hide his features as he executed a schoolboy. His last word, muffled by black wool, came out thick and quiet. 'Sorry.'

A spasm of terror went through Elliot. He pulled back hard on the grid of metal and something extraordinary happened. The whole thing suddenly lurched up, like the lid of a box. It was heavy and unwieldy but it pivoted cleanly from the bottom edge, right by his firmly planted feet. It swung upwards with an up-fling of water weed and pond algae which spattered across the gunman's black-clad chest.

But more usefully, one of its thin rods caught the shot intended for Elliot. For the second time in less than 15 minutes he had literally dodged a bullet. This one deflected and punched through the glass of an upper storey classroom window. The gunman cursed and then laughed, shaking his head, as Elliot hauled the shallow metal cage fully upright in front of him, like the world's most inadequate shield. He stood behind it, panting, holding the corners in a death grip, as his legs threatened to buckle beneath him. If his assailant had been throwing football sized missiles it might have helped, but it wasn't much use against a highly trained sniper with .2mm bullets. He had probably just won himself another ten seconds of life.

'Seriously - you are a trier!' chuckled the man. 'It does seem a shame to knock you out so young. Can't be helped though.'

'You're an arse!' shouted back Elliot. Where this had come from he had no clue. But he had nothing much to lose. He shrieked a few more insults which would have done Shania proud and the man laughed even louder and then stepped into the pond to wade across closer to him. 'The next shot will be point blank. You won't suffer,' he said, taking aim, heedless of the water sloshing around his knees.

Elliot gave it his best and last. With his final curse he shoved the pond cover back at his killer. It toppled over squarely, and Elliot rode the fall, still tightly gripping the metal rods. At his end the grid was still attached; the whole thing designed to open up on a hinge. It hit the gunman hard on the brow. He was pole-axed, backwards, into the water. Elliot, two inches away, watched the dark eyes widen in surprise and then fill with water as they were plunged beneath the surface.

The water churned frenziedly as the man found himself engulfed in its half metre depth. Almost immediately his face bloomed back up, surrounded by sodden black wool, but could get no higher than a nose-length above the surface, pressed down by the metal grid and the weight of the schoolboy on top of it.

Elliot stared down in shock. Had he just got the better of his killer? It seemed like it. The man tried to launch himself up out of the water again, pushing the grid off him. As strong as he was, he just couldn't get enough leverage from his awkward angle, flat on his back and wallowing in water, his thick black clothing soaked and dragging.

Elliot realized this was the moment to run... but if he got off the grid his weight would no longer be holding it down and the man would be out in seconds and after him, firing. Or maybe not. What had become of the gun? Did Jonah still have it? Was he about to get a bullet in the belly? No - the man was now plunging back down and grappling around with both hands below the surface. He must have dropped it! Elliot grinned. He knew how soupy, weedy and clogged the bottom of this pond was. The state of that Year 7 when he'd finally pulled him out! A heavy gun would be deep in that stew by now. Not easily found.

Now was the time to go, but first there was one more thing he could try. Slowly, he crawled over the imprisoned killer, bouncing on the juddering metal grid as the man fought on in a fresh surge to get out. A brief pause followed as he sank under again and began scrabbling once more for his weapon.

Elliot reached across the narrow concrete path and grabbed the foot of the wrought iron bench. It was not designed to be moved. It shouldn't have been possible, but the adrenalin flashing through him powered his muscles in ways he could not have imagined. Keeping his body weight central, Elliot tugged the bench with all his strength as, once again, the grid bucked and rode underneath him, giving way to the force of the strong man in the pond.

'OH... NO...' grunted Elliot, his arms screaming with protest, 'YOU... DON'T!'

He stood up after the bench was fully in place. It was heavy. So heavy its movement had left scrape marks across the concrete. A grown man could drag it sideways but there was no way he could lift it off him from beneath. Not while pinned under a metal grid in a pond, straining to breathe through nostrils barely clear of the water.

Elliot stamped down on the grid and let out a wild shout of laughter. Then he ran for the door, further along the quad. As he reached it he turned back to watch for nearly a minute. The bench juddered repeatedly but did not shift. The man's fingers, pale in the thin light, were clenched on the metal grid, as Elliot's had been five minutes earlier. But fingers were all Elliot could see. Was he drowning? He didn't need to. If he could just hold on and keep calm his nose and mouth would clear the surface. If he kept struggling, though, he might drown himself in his own tidal wave. The odd gurgling cry came from the water but it was swamped every time.

Elliot decided he did not care whether Jonah drowned or not. He just had to get out of school.

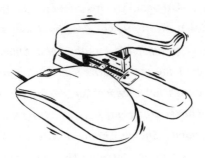

Feed

Shania's attacker smelled of disinfectant. She felt his long hair against her face and this thin body striking hers. And realized he was a mop.

The mop clattered to the floor as she got to her feet, gasping. She glanced quickly around and worked out she was in the caretaker's office. It was a small room built on a split level, off the stairwell which connected the ground, first and second floors. It had wooden shelving from floor to ceiling, filled with boxes of paper towels, toilet roll, bars of soap and bottles of disinfectant. A narrow window let in a little light from a half moon just rising in the evening sky. Did she dare turn on the light? No. There was a glass pane in the door which led out onto the stairwell. She couldn't risk it.

She waited for her heartbeat to stop bashing through her throat and ears and tried to calm down. She took long, slow breaths, the way that dozy woman at the anger management course had suggested. She heard again the instructions she had been given in that annoying, wifty-wafty voice. *'Breathe iiiiiiiin, through the nose. Breathe oooooout through the mouth. Good, Shania. Gooood! Now clench your whole body and breathe iiiiiin.... then breathe oooooout! And release the clench! Releeeeeease! Can you feel the release? Let all the bad feelings and anger drop away from you. Drop them. Drop them all! Good, Shania. Goood... Shania. Shania. Please put that down. Please. No - don't drop that! It's quite valuable. No... no, that doesn't need to be released! Stop it! Stop it at ONCE! Oh - you little animal!'*

She laughed, remembering the woman's face going from faked serenity to blotchy fury. She hadn't actually dropped her precious vase anyway. She had just thought about it. And it was a valid experiment. If Cassandra Le Guin was claiming to be able to teach her how to de-stress and control anger, it was useful to find out whether Cassandra Le Guin could apply those same techniques to herself. Turns out, no.

But actually, the technique wasn't all that bad. It seemed to be helping now. The slow breathing in and out did regulate her freaked out heart and take the thudding out of her head. Now she could hear if anybody was outside on the stairwell. It seemed like nobody was.

So... where was the best escape route? If she went down the stairs, which were concrete, with solid walls on either side, she wouldn't be able to see anyone coming up from below or down from above – not until they could see her. She would be effectively blind until she'd turned the corner on each level.

She frowned and closed her eyes, picturing the lay-out of the building. She was in a room halfway between the ground floor and the upper floor. Upper floor was all Year 7 and 8 classrooms, with the science labs at one end and a small kitchen for Food Science classes (cookery, in other words). Shania would never admit it out loud but she quite liked doing cookery. She loved the smell of baking cakes and bread.

What else was on the upper floor? Yes. The head teacher' office. And a *landline phone*. Would it be working? Or cut off? She couldn't guess but there was another good reason to go there, anyway. The head's office had a fire escape. She could get out. She just had to go up the stairwell and along the corridor without meeting an assassin. *Come on, she urged herself. Avoiding people who make you dead inside – you do that every day.*

Or she could just stay here. Hide under the caretaker's table. But no. She couldn't, any more than she could have stayed in the crawl space beneath her feet. She had to DO something. Sitting around passively was just not her style: one of the main reasons she was such a nightmare in school.

She took a deep breath and slowly opened the door onto the stairwell, her ears straining for the slightest sound above or below. Nothing. Silence. Apart from her own heart, once again thudding in her ears. She slid outside and gently closed the door behind her.

The rubber soles of her Doc Martens were quiet as she crept up the stairs. She thought she heard a splinter of glass at one point, but it was obviously some distance away. She went on up, marshalling her breathing and trying to keep it steady and quiet. On the top floor the dim corridor stretched away to her left and her right and she immediately headed left, to the head teacher's office. She'd been there enough times to know where it was. She kept close to the shadowy wall, resisting the urge to move across and peer out of the windows and down into the quad when she thought she heard someone cry out. She couldn't look. She might see something. But something might see her.

She reached the office in less than a minute and tried the door. It wasn't locked. Inside was a small lobby containing the secretary's desk and cupboard and the next door along led into Gallagher's room. It was dark and silent but she could make out the shape of his desk and the phone resting on it. Her night vision had become pretty sharp over the last hour. She snatched up the handset, desperate for the burring sound of a live landline. But the phone was silent. Of course it was. Like Elliot had said, they'd cut off communications. Not power though – because the light had been on in the classroom while they'd been taking their test. Someone must have been carefully and selectively snipping connections. What about the fire alarm? She glanced around and located the little plastic box on the wall, a glint of thin glass protecting the alarm trigger. She could smash it now and set off all the alarms – bring the emergency services running.

She picked up a heavy stapler from the desk, pulled it back in her fist, and then and drove it hard into the glass. The glass shattered on impact. Then the ear-splitting shriek of an alarm bell... entirely failed to occur. Shania sank into the chair by the desk, hope and energy draining from her. Obviously the careful wire-snipping guy had got this covered too. It would have to be the fire escape. Going outside and down an obvious, signposted escape route, though, was not a happy thought. The man patrolling outside might easily spot her doing that and – stuck on a ladder – she'd have nowhere to hide.

Her slumped, defeated form was reflecting in a flat screen monitor. At the base of the monitor a pinprick of green light was pulsing. So... there was power to the head teacher's PC. Maybe she could log on and get help that way. Through email or - or Facebook or Twitter or something. Even as she started booting up the machine she was laughing at herself. Who, in their right mind, was ever going read a desperate plea for help on social media from Shania Laker and take it seriously?

Help me! I'm being chased round my school by masked gunmen! #crap-goingtodie.

She'd probably get about 50 likes or re-tweets, mind.

But... maybe there was a website for the local police? She'd heard about the police trying to interact with the community online. That might work – an emergency email to the local cop shop.

Idiot. The moment she logged on, using her student ID, she was brought up sharp. There were enough safeguards to stop her getting out on the internet anyway – this was *school* for god's sake - but she'd thought she might work around those. And she might – if the connection wasn't completely dead. And it was. Every attempt she made to reach the worldwide web met with the message: **UNABLE TO OPEN PAGE: CHECK YOUR CONNECTION** and an endlessly swirly little blue circle, going nowhere. Much like her. Well, *dur*, Shania. The broadband was probably even in the same *fibre optic wire* as the telephone. Shania head-butted the keyboard in frustration and then heard a ***BING***.

Glancing up she realized she had activated something with her face. The screen had split into four equal sized rectangles. In each of these was a grey image of some part of the school. She had nutted an icon and opened the school's security camera feed. And in it she saw Elliot. He was still alive!

And he was about to die. Again.

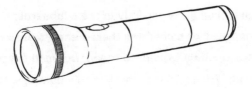

Last Life

Elliot ran down the corridor. Again. In the dark. Again. In fear of his life. Again. This was feeling more and more like an all-nighter on the XBox. Except that pulling an all-nighter on the Xbox was fun. And this was as far from fun as it was possible to be.

Also, on the XBox, he was always thoroughly weaponed up and had several lives to lose. Here he was unarmed and dead meant dead. Game over. His score was low; he was carrying nothing useful. Your average secondary school didn't offer much in the way of weaponry but as he ran, crouching low in the shadows, he wondered what he might use, if he ended up in another combat situation. Trapping Jonah in the pond had given him back just one glowing bar of energy. He had won a level. He'd just about escaped Cain - the first guy in Level One, thanks to Zombie Gallagher – and then he'd met a boss at the end of Level Two. And beaten him all by himself.

So now what? Find another classroom with a window facing *out* this time. But also... weapon up? What could he use?

There was stuff in the science labs which could do some harm... but it was all locked away securely in the cupboards. The kitchen? A knife? He might find something there but he feared the kitchen area was also securely locked. He needed *something* to throw or swing or... wait. Elliot paused, checking his bearings. What about the gym cupboard? There were shot putts and javelins in there. He felt a smile pucker his face (an alien sensation after the past hour). Yes... he could turn around and go back to the gym and get some stuff to use as defence!

Against a bullet? said a cold voice in his head.

Fair point. He shook his head. No. He had to get to the end of this corridor and turn right and then go into any one of the classrooms in this part of the school. They all had windows opening onto the outer grounds of the school. He needed to get out of here. Briefly he thought about Shania. If he was heroic he would be looking for her first... but he wasn't heroic and besides, she had probably already got out. She would have escaped as soon as he'd fallen through the ceiling and created a distraction.

The T junction of corridors was only a few feet away. Get there. Get around the corner. Get to the classrooms. Get out through the windows. Get out. Get out. Get out.

Then he saw the blue beams of light. Two beams, intersecting, from opposite directions, like long, thin, silent light sabres. The men wielding the lights were seconds away. This must be the men who had been upstairs. They must have finished and come back down to find Jonah and Cain. They would meet at the T junction and, having swept the corridors and rooms, swing around and continue together in one direction. Right towards him. He grabbed the first door he could find and shot inside. Right into a stationery cupboard.

It was as good as pressing the QUIT button. He had just backed himself into a corner. There was no way out. How likely was it that they would fail to check a cupboard? And with the door shut, he could no longer see the blue beams. He had no idea how close they were.

Elliot sank to the floor of the cupboard. His energy bar was flashing red. It was nearly game over.

QUIT? Are you sure you want to QUIT without SAVING?

It would probably be quick, at least. They were professionals. Instant bullet to the forehead. Done. All very tidy. Only a very random bit of chance could possibly save him now, and after the zombie intervention and the bullet deflecting off the pond grid, he must have used up all his lives by now. He was dead.

The Scream

Shania watched as Elliot ran along the corridor, stooped low. Even through the grainy grey of the camera feed she knew it was him by the way he moved and the fuzzy dark crop of hair. Wearing a white school shirt also helped to pick him out pretty clearly. Bad choice of colour. But then the school uniform options probably didn't feature a 'totally black in case of attempted assassination' range.

Maybe he would get out, she thought. But a second later she knew he wouldn't, because in another feed she could see two dark figures stalking determinedly along at opposite ends of the corridor Elliot was running towards. The camera flipped around every few seconds, allowing her to see both men approaching in sudden time-lapse leaps. Very shortly they would meet, turn and continue together down the corridor which Elliot was in.

Elliot knew this too. She could tell by the way he'd suddenly frozen to the spot. There was no audio on the security feed. It all looked like a badly directed silent movie. Shania felt sick. She knew what the next scene would be: Elliot getting shot. Probably in the back of the head as he stumbled away.

But no – he wasn't running. He'd decided to hide. He'd thrown himself through a door. She groaned out loud. Why hadn't he run back another few steps and opened the door to the classroom? The loser had gone into a *cupboard!* They'd open it! He was a sitting duck.

And now the men had met at the T junction of the corridors and were turning in the direction of the cupboard, first kicking open the door to a classroom. One went in while the other stood at the threshold, glancing up and down the corridor, his rifle resting back along his upper arm and shoulder. Shania screamed aloud with frustration. They were seconds away from discovering Elliot. If only she could distract them!

Then she realized that she could. There was a microphone on the desk, to the left of the monitor. And she knew what it did. It was the school tannoy. Better than that... it worked in parts of the school. The head teacher was such a control freak he wanted to be able to tannoy the gym without interrupting an assembly. Or announce stuff in the dining hall without messing up the atmosphere of lessons.

All this she knew because she'd been in here, getting told off, so many times. She'd seen him use it. The four buttons at the base of the microphone - a small barrel shaped thing on a flexible metal neck - were labelled. Shania just about made out DINING HALL. She rammed her finger into the button and screamed.

'HEEEEEEEEEEEEELP! HEEEEEEEEEEELP ME! OH GOD, SOMEBODY, PLEEEEASE, PLEASE COME! PLEASE HELP ME! THEY'RE TRYING TO KILL ME!'

The effect was electrifying. The black figures jolted and spun around in the direction of the screaming. It was coming from the dining hall, further along the corridor, well away from Elliot's hiding place. Once they got there it would be obvious the screaming was coming from speakers up on the wall – but from this distance they couldn't tell. It *could* be from someone actually at that location.

The men did not wait to query the acoustic quality of Shania's banshee wailing – and she was giving it the full punk girl screech now; simply opening her throat and letting it all out. They sprinted along the corridor, leaving Elliot undiscovered in the cupboard. Shania kept screaming a little longer. She poured all of her very real panic into the performance. And then she went suddenly silent. She hoped it would seem as if she had heard or seen the gunmen coming. Hopefully she had cut out the microphone before they'd actually arrived, so they wouldn't hear the tell-tale buzz from the dated old PA system and immediately guess it was a trick.

Now... Elliot. Would he *know* it was safe to leave the cupboard? She stared at the door for five seconds, *willing* him to get out. But nothing moved. 'HICKMAN! YOU IDIOT!' she cursed. 'DON'T MAKE ME COME DOWN THERE!' She was already moving, though, and in moments was sprinting along the top corridor and down to the stairwell. Even in the dark she knew where she was going. This was something she had over their attackers, at least. She knew this godawful school like the back of her hand. She arrived in the corridor in half a minute, panting hard, and wrenched open the cupboard door to find Elliot cowering inside. She didn't say anything; she just grabbed his arm and dragged him out. Then she dragged him a bit further as he slowly came out of his paralysis and seemed to work out what was happening. *'RUN!'* she hissed. *'THIS WAY!'*

They made a lot of noise, panting and gasping and slapping their feet hard on the concrete stairwell. For all she knew, another pair of killers could be waiting at the top. But she couldn't stop running.

Less than 90 seconds after she'd left Gallagher's office, she was back in it, with Elliot in tow. He collapsed onto the floor, spluttering and heaving. She realized he was being sick.

'Nice,' she said, leaning back on the desk, arms folded.

'What happened?' he gurgled, on his hands and knees. 'They were coming for me. Why didn't they open the door? I heard them coming!'

'Didn't you hear the shrieking?' asked Shania.

He sat up, rocking back against his heels and holding his face, his brown skin washed grey by the half moon light from outside He looked like a painting. *The Scream*, maybe, thought Shania.

'I did hear shrieking,' he said, faintly. 'I thought it was me.'

'Nah,' she said, grinning. 'That was me. I give good shriek. Souxsie and The Banshees could only dream of the Shania Shriek. Did it through the tannoy to the dining hall, so they'd go there instead of finding you.'

He stared at her.

'Well, don't feel you have to thank me,' she muttered.

'Sh-Shania...' he burbled, rocking slightly and still holding his face. 'I saw Gallagher... he... he came back.'

'What? What are you talking about? He's dead,' she said flatly, trying to bat away the big lump of freaked-out unreality which threatened to engulf her when she pictured her head teacher on the floor. Some of his blood was on her sleeve.

'I know,' said Elliot. 'He's still dead. But... he came back.'

Oh great. Now he was losing it. Shania stared at him for a few seconds and then shook her head. 'Look – forget about zombie Gallagher,' she said. 'There are *real live* gunmen out there – and they won't be fooled for long,' she said. 'Even if they didn't work out it was just the PA.'

Elliot gulped. 'Shania... what if they *did* work out it was the PA?'

There was a pause. Shania took in his meaning. These men had been very, very organized. They had studied the lay out of the building and the habits of the staff. It was quite likely they would know where the tannoy announcements came from. Reception. And here.

Even as she thought this, movement from the security screens caught her eye. The two men in black were on the move again. They were heading for the stairwell she and Elliot had just climbed. If they knew where they were going, they were roughly 30 seconds away.

A pitch in the dark

'The fire escape!' said Elliot and they both ran for the emergency exit door on the far side of Gallagher's office. Elliot shoved down hard on the metal bar and it opened with a loud clunk. It should have set off the alarm but nothing rang out. Outside was a short, steep open stairwell which led up to the roof of the building. Pushing the door behind them closed, they climbed quickly. The metal treads rang out like chime bars. It felt, thought Elliot, like every part of this school wanted them caught. Except, maybe, the fishpond. He felt a remote flash of pride in that. He wondered if the guy had got out yet. Or if he'd drowned.

At the top of the stairs Elliot glanced around. They were on a flat roof, spanning the long, thin rectangle of the block, a waist height brick wall around its perimeter. Heating vents and air conditioning ducts grew out of the old tarred surface here and there like random mushrooms and a cluster of satellite dishes and antennae occupied one far corner. There were also several metal gas flues and a tall, skinny brick stack – a hangover from the 1960s design when a chimney for the school kitchen was a necessity.

More importantly, across the low wall in three places around the roof there were metal rungs and arched handrails. Shania ran to the nearest and peered over the edge, gripping the hand rails. 'How does this thing work?' she hissed, glancing back at the little stairwell they'd come up through with fear etched on her face. She didn't look keen to use it. Elliot didn't blame her. They were horribly exposed; their white school shirts positively glowing against the black rooftop. He leaned over and examined the emergency escape ladder. It was aluminium; very light. It was made up of four connected ladders, contracted and stacked up together, ready to slide out in stages towards the ground. To make this happen you needed to push down and twist two orange levers. The mechanism was stiff – it had probably not been used for years. Elliot pushed and twisted, grunting with the effort, while Shania stood, staring left and right and up and down, like a very scared punk meerkat. 'They'll be here any second!' she whimpered.

At *last* the mechanism gave and the ladders extended. GOOD!

BAD! They made the most unholy screeching cacophony Elliot had ever heard. Shania probably *had* heard worse, being into punk, but nothing could prepare either of them for the sheer horror of this noise. It split the night like a chainsaw duelling a jackhammer – *Screeee-shuunk!!! Screeee-shuunk!!! Screeee-shuunk!!! Screeee-shuunk!!!*

'What the hell does the caretaker get paid for?!' wailed Shania. 'Hasn't he heard of WD40?'

Elliot took a microsecond to be impressed that Shania knew what WD40 was before grabbing her arm and running to the far side of the roof. Someone had emerged around the corner of the grounds below them – someone with a blue-beamed torch, swinging upward. And he could also hear, in the quiet that followed the ladders' final tumbling shriek, the door to the stairwell thudding open. He made for the satellite dishes – the only other thing up here glowing as white as they were.

They skidded behind the dishes seconds before two men arrived on the roof. Shania let out a low moan. He guessed she was feeling pretty much the way he had as he sat in that store cupboard. Preparing for the end. He guessed it really was over this time.

Yet it seemed they'd be getting the full, final cliffhanger treatment because the men had set off towards the ladder, seen that it had no hyperventilating teenager clinging to it, and then split up to walk slowly around the perimeter, parallel to each other. They held their guns at the ready as their torch beams swept efficiently left and right; stretching out their prey's agonizing final moments.

Elliot's brain was doing backflips, trying to find some way out. He located the other two ladder escapes. One was in the diagonal corner, the furthest away from them. Another was closer, to their right, slightly in the shadow of the old skinny chimney stack. If he could get to that point, unnoticed... it was only another short sprint back to the stairwell. But how likely was that? With both men working the perimeter, walking right towards them, and his shirt like a white flare... it would just make the whole thing more fun for them; that's all. Elliot closed his eyes – and then opened them and then prodded Shania's foot. 'Give me your boot!' he hissed.

'What?' she croaked.

'I need one of your boots. Right now.'

She stared at him for a moment, baffled. 'First the zombie thing... now this..?' she murmured. 'And whoa – now the boy's ripping his shirt off! Look, Hickman, I know we're going to die but I don't want to get kinky with you!'

'Shut up and get your boot off!' he grunted, shrugging out of his sleeves. Mercifully Shania shut up and did what he asked. By the time he had the slightly warm, sweaty Doc Marten in his fist, the gunmen were halfway down the roof towards them. Ten more seconds and he wouldn't have a hope of pulling this off. Elliot stood up behind the satellite dish, stuffed his bunched up white shirt down his trousers out of sight, and swung the boot round and round by its long laces, building up velocity. Then – at the right moment, he released – and the shiny black missile went sailing through the air. His aim was good. It struck a bin-lid shaped metal vent at the far end of the roof. The metallic clang had both men spinning around in an instant but not before the boot had come to rest, out of sight.

'In the vent!' called one and they ran back towards it, one

communicating this latest intel to the man downstairs with his radio. 'Kid's in the vent. We've got him.'

'Stay here!' hissed Elliot and then ran for the ladder. Without his shirt there was only a faint gleam of moonlight on his brown skin. And his dark grey trousers and black trainers reflected no light at all. He reached the ladder and pulled his shirt out of his trousers, dropping it over the edge, where it fluttered down to the bushes below like a giant, drunken moth. Then he twisted the levers. These gave more easily and suddenly the air was filled with *Screeee-shuunk!!! Screeee-shuunk!!! Screeee-shuunk!!! Screeee-shuunk!!!*

But the moment it gave off its horrific alarm call, Elliot ducked down and ran to the chimney.

The gunmen, peering into the empty vent, spun around and gave a shout. 'Ladder! South wall! South wall!' one called into the two-way as they ran for the second emergency escape route.

Elliot flattened himself against the brick stack. It was barely wide enough to hide him. He carefully eased around it, out of sight, as they approached the ladder. 'Could he have got down there?' asked one. 'That fast?'

'Looks like he lost his shirt on the way,' said the other and the first one began to climb down the extended ladder while his comrade radioed in the latest. Elliot took a lungful of air and then ran for the stairwell. As he reached the metal treads he knew he could do nothing about the chime bars ringing out again – but in any case, he needed to make some noise if he was going to get them off the roof and away from Shania. Getting them to give chase was the only way.

They didn't miss much. The shouts were up again the minute he hit the top step and the one who'd climbed halfway down the ladder was back up again in seconds. But Elliot was through the door into Gallagher's room by then, skidding briefly on his own vomit before sprinting across the lobby and along the corridor at a speed which wouldn't have shamed him at an Olympic try out. He just hoped Shania would rub her two brain cells together and work out what he was doing and why. She had a much better chance of making it off the roof now.

Would she have the sense to take that chance before one of the gunmen remembered he'd not reached the satellite dishes and went back to finish the job?

Flare

Behind the satellite dish Shania stared at her remaining boot and felt a wash of clammy horror roll over her. He'd left her! He'd just run away – saved his own skin! Then she heard the clang of the steps and the loud thud of the door back into Gallagher's office and thought maybe... just maybe... he'd done that for her.

As the two gunmen raced across the roof towards him she understood that this was another chance. A good chance. If they were chasing down Elliot she might have a hope of getting away this time. A terrible weariness descended on her. Seconds ago her whole body had been clenched, thrumming, pounding, arteries squirting blood around to her brain and heart at jet hose-pressure levels. Her mind had been in a free-fall of terror. She had fully expected to be dead by now.

And she wasn't.

Her limbs felt like lead. She wanted to sleep.

She was probably going into shock. Actual shock, this time.

Shania swore at herself. She told herself exactly what she thought of herself. She very nearly smacked herself in the face for being so pathetic. Seriously? Was she really going to let some macho testosterone freaks in James Bond baddie outfits have the last word?

She got to her feet unsteadily and limped across the roof to find her boot, staying away from the walls in case torchy-boy down in the grounds saw her blonde hair or her white shirt. The boot lay on its side against a steel gas flue and she felt a tiny measure of comfort as she laced it back on. And a tiny measure of respect for Elliot, for using it as a missile; for working out a plan when she'd been too paralyzed to think. Had he saved her life twice now? She'd only saved his once. If she got off this roof and ran away, nobody would be counting. They might already have him; it might already be over. She'd never even the score. That would be bad. But dying would be worse. If she went over the wall she might get unlucky and the patrolling sniper might see her. But if she stayed up here they'd soon come back. They must know there was more than one student in the building now, thanks to her PA trick. She had blown her own cover. Unless they thought Elliot screamed like a girl... and really, he didn't. Above her, stars were prickling coldly through the dark sky and far away in the distance she heard sirens. Too far away.

'Police!' she sighed. 'Always there when I *don't* need you. And now, the one time I do...'

Normally she attracted cops like a dropped Cornetto attracts ants. She'd done all the right things; stealing from shops, getting into fights, creating a disturbance, vandalism, arson. Yeah. Do all that and you get to know the local cop shop quite well.

But where's a policeman when you need one?

She walked quietly back across the roof and the tiny flame of an idea lit up her darkened mind. 'Shania...' she marvelled at herself. 'You're a maniac!'

Kit

'Where the hell is Jonah?'

Elliot pressed himself deeper into the pile of coats, blazers and old PE kit and tried not to think about whose sock was tickling his nose. The clothing muffled his breathing and he lay still, like a rabbit beneath a hovering raptor. His predators were in the wide lobby that led to reception and their prey was hidden just around a corner in a pile of lost property, three or four metres away.

He heard them try to raise Jonah. And then Cain. Neither man responded.

'Goliath,' grunted the boss man – calling himself David, if Elliot's messed up brain could still remember correctly – 'We may have two men down and one dead man walking.' He let off a series of hissed expletives. 'And one teenager somewhere in the building. Possibly two. Set up an electronic perimeter. NOBODY leaves this school until I have decided *how*.'

Goliath's compressed radio voice came back: 'I can't raise Cain or Jonah either. But nobody has left the building. I set up the trips as soon as I saw movement in the girls' toilets. Nothing has gone off since then. Nobody has come out – not any kids and not Gallagher.'

'We split up,' said David to Abel. 'You take the east wing and I'll take the west. Damn. We needed more men!'

'You said five was more than enough to take out one guy,' pointed out Abel.

'And it would have been if Cain had been the hotshot you told me he was,' snapped back David. 'I depend on you to bring in the best and what do I get?'

'He *is* the best I know,' replied Abel. 'It was a random element. A fox.'

'And the kid in detention – that was another random element, was it?'

Abel started to defend himself again but David cut in. 'Enough. We can do this later. You take east, I'll take west – we work back to the central staircase, go up together and then repeat. We finish this, we find Gallagher and the boy – and anyone skulking in this building - we dispatch them and we get out of here.'

They departed rapidly and Elliot lay under the lost property for a minute or more, astonished that neither of them had turned around and kicked their way through the pile of clothing next to the lockers. He had found a small mountain of it against the large plastic crate it was kept in. Clearly the men had been through the box on an earlier sweep. He couldn't get into the crate and pull the clothing on top of him – they'd probably notice that. So he'd thrown half the clothes into a couple of open lockers and jammed them shut and then lay down against the canvas crate, pulling the rest of the gear on top of him and hoping it looked much the same as they'd left it. It had taken him about thirty seconds to work all this out and do it, knowing they were close behind him. Moments after he'd pulled the last sweaty rugby shirt over his face they had reached the lobby and paused for their radio exchange.

He still couldn't believe it had worked. The pile he had recreated must have looked convincingly like the one they'd created themselves. It was another amazingly lucky break – but it might be his last. They were sweeping again and one of them – Abel, probably, would be back again shortly. So – what to do?

His success with Shania's boot had given him one more little glowing bar of energy and self-belief. A missile to throw had been good. He needed more of those. He thought again about the gym. If Abel was going back to the east wing and David to the west, would either of them also re-sweep the gym – off on its little spur corridor? That was on David's wing and yeah – he probably would. But when? There was the dining hall to check as well and he couldn't walk in two different directions at once. Truth was, he didn't have enough men left to do this properly. There was every chance he would turn across to the dining hall and the kitchens first and then go down to the gym – and if so, that would offer some valuable moments for a boy to get to the games cupboard and find a javelin.

Elliot sat up and grabbed a black zip up hoodie from the pile of lost property. It fit him well enough and made him feel less vulnerable than running around topless like a calendar model. ***MR OCTOBER: Elliot likes to stay fit by outrunning masked gunmen, stripped to the waist!*** He zipped up the top and pulled the hood up. Then he pushed it down again. He needed to hear everything. He also needed to make no noise. He surveyed his trainers and then, reluctantly, took them off. They were quiet enough normally but one tiny squeak on the tiled floor could mean the end of him. With bare feet he could run with stealth.

He emerged from the lobby, glancing left and right, keeping low. There were flickers of torchlight in both directions, but both moving away from him. He turned left and ran after David. Breathing through his mouth, silently, his bare feet made next to no noise and the cool tiles beneath them gave him a sensation of heightened reality. He felt connected to the ground; his heart rate was fast but not out of control; every sinew in his body was singing with anticipation. Terror had given away to grim determination.

He was gaining on David; one dark figure chasing another. If he'd had a javelin or a rounders bat with him now he might even have tried to get the man from behind; but he did not. Not yet. Ahead of him David reached the junction with the corridor that went left, down into the gym and the double doors to the right, opening into the dining hall and the school kitchens beyond. The man paused, considering, sweeping the torch around. Elliot dropped flat to the floor in the shadow of a trolley of exercise books and project folders. He managed it with no noise, amazing himself. He held his breath;

thinking his lungs into concrete. For what seemed like minutes on end, David paused. Then, just as Elliot's concrete lungs were about to shatter, the man opted to go into the dining hall.

As soon as the double doors swung shut again, a blast of exhaled air powered Elliot up and along and to the left. His feet slapped rapidly on the corridor floor and then he was through the double doors into the gym, catching them just in time to stop them swinging back and thudding noisily together. The gym was dark and silent, as before. Elliot sprinted across it and climbed the bars, up to where he and Shania had clung what seemed like hours ago. From the top he could see through the high windows and make out the dim shape of the 4x4 which was still blocking the exit doors outside. Fine. He hadn't expected any different. And judging by what Goliath had been saying, there was some kind of electronic surveillance perimeter set up around the whole building. Wherever he went now, he was going to trip a beam and alert the gunmen. Then it was just a case of whether he could outrun them.

The school was surrounded by sports fields, a wide car park and netball and basketball courts. And around the grounds were a lot of trees – but they were distant; at least 30 seconds' hard run away. Could he get across the exposed area and into those trees before he got shot? He had no idea. And right now, running wasn't on his mind. Right now, fighting back was the best option.

He got down and crossed the floor to the games cupboard. Inside, he pulled the door shut behind him before feeling around for the light switch. The yellow flare of bulb-light was dazzling. He'd been operating in the semi-dark for so long now, his eyes had gone nocturnal. He blinked a few times, alarmed at the idea of the light seeping out under the door just as David arrived for another sweep. He needed to find what he'd come for fast.

There were racks of hula hoops and thick shiny tumbling mats stacked as high as his waist. And in crates he found bean bags and balls of all kinds – tennis, pingpong, cricket, football... Hung up on pegs were drawstring kit bags and stretchy vinyl bands used in yoga and pilates – the keep fit stuff girls liked to do. There were lightweight plastic cricket and rounders stumps and bails - but no bats. There were rolls of mesh for table tennis and weighted stands and nets for badminton, along with tube after tube of shuttle cocks. But no racquets. Elliot groaned. He picked up a table tennis bat. Maybe if the bad guy stood still long enough he could inflict death by a thousand ping-pongs.

It was a well-stocked cupboard. But not well stocked enough. There wasn't a single javelin in it either. Elliot Hickman slumped onto the mats and cursed a loser student he knew well. Elliot Hickman. Because - yes - he had brought this on himself. Last term he had been caught fighting Aaron Miller - martial arts style - with two cricket bats. Nobody had got hurt. It was just a game. But Mr Rayner had gone nuclear about the whole thing and after a week of detention, the next time Elliot looked into the games store cupboard he found all the bats and racquets missing. They were now securely locked in a different cupboard in Mr Rayner's office, along with the javelins. Was this karma? wondered Elliot. All his bad behaviour chickens coming home to roost? Cosmic payback? Whatever you wanted to call it, he was screwed.

So. Now what? David must have swept the dining room by now. He'd be heading to the gym – arriving any second. He would of course go for the cupboard again. Was there time to get out before then? To go back to the bars, climb up and hope that once again his enemy would not look up? No. They'd got away with it before because the men had not been seriously searching the place. They had believed, at that point, that all they needed to do was retrieve one body and then split. Not now. David did not sound like the kind of man who wouldn't figure out that looking UP was an option.

Even as he thought this he heard a distant thud. David was on his way down the corridor the gym. Elliot gulped. Had he just backed himself into a certain death corner *again?*

Not if he could help it. He looked at the heavily weighted tennis net stands and the cricket gear. And then at the yoga bands. It might not be as good as the javelin plan, but it was better than nothing.

He picked up a band and stretched it. He lifted the metal stand in one fist. He filled a drawstring PE bag and slung it over one shoulder. Then he switched off the light and got into position. He might be about to die but not without a fight. He had the stand; he had stretchy yoga bands... and he had balls.

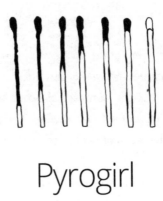

Pyrogirl

Finding wooden stuff wasn't easy. Everything was plastic or metal or flame retardant MDF. Shania had a bin full of paper but that wasn't enough. Paper was only the kindling. It would be gone in seconds.

Eventually she found something that would burn – a small wooden table on high legs which stood in the corner of the secretary's lobby area, holding up a pot plant. Shania dumped the plant on the floor and then, glancing carefully around the crack of the door, checked that there was no dark masked figure within listening distance. She could see nobody, so she swung the high table thing by its legs and cracked it against the desk until it broke into several splintery bits. Excellent.

She carried the wood and her bin of paper kindling back to the head's office, digging a small plastic lighter out of her skirt pocket. Shania didn't smoke but she liked to have a source of flame available to her. She hadn't tried to set fire to anything or anyone for well over a year but just knowing she possessed a little shiny casket of lighter fluid with its own built in sparking device made her feel slightly less angry about life. Just slightly.

Of course, if it was ever found on her she'd be suspended from school – or even excluded permanently. Not carrying matches or a lighter had been part of the 'contract' she'd scribbled her name on last year, after the incident with Mr Fawkes. Seriously, though, with a name like that – how you *not* set fire to him?!

OK. She knew it was bad. But she hadn't really set fire to him – or ever intended to. It was just a joke. Mr Fawkes had kept her in at lunchtime because she'd been chewing gum. When he'd asked her to spit it out she'd told him that research suggested people could concentrate better in class when they were chewing – it was a scientific fact.

'I don't care if Professor Stephen Hawking told you to chew that stuff – I won't have it in my class,' Mr Fawkes had snapped. 'Cut the attitude and spit it out.' So she had. On his shoes.

He made her sit by his desk, writing lines, as everyone else went off for lunch. She was hungry. He was denying her lunch. He sat there with his copy of the Telegraph and held it up to read so he didn't have to look at her whenever she glared at him. Shania liked being ignored even less than she liked being told what to do. So she got out her lighter and quietly set fire to his newspaper.

How was she to know Fawkes was such a panicky guy? And that he'd be stupid enough to start flailing it about in the air so that it set off the school smoke alarms. Seriously – didn't teachers know *anything* about how to put out a flame?! In the end she'd had to shout at him to put it in the metal bin by his desk. And *she* dumped a fire blanket on it and put it out. The whole school filed outside and got 25 minutes off lessons. She got suspended for a week. It was only because she'd acted fast and put it out that she avoided getting an interview with the police.

Anyway. That was then. And if the smoke alarms were working now, she'd be delighted. She could hold up her lighter and set them off, but she'd already tried that and... nothing.

As she passed back through the room she caught movement on the security camera feed and saw one of the gunmen working his way across the dining hall, slanting his torch beam left and right. Then, in a corridor, she made out another dark figure. It was moving differently... kind of... staggering. Was that *Elliot*? Wounded? No... it was bigger, more broad-shouldered and...

Shania dropped her splintered wood and stifled a cry with both hands. She had not believed Elliot when he'd said it. She'd thought he was in shock or maybe concussed and just babbling. But right there, lurching across the screen, was the unmistakable figure of Mr Gallagher. She recognized his tweedy jacket. Their head teacher was back from the dead! She felt a cold shiver shoot up through her and send goosebumps all over her skin. *No. No no no no!* How could this *be?* Zombies did NOT exist...

...but Gallagher's brains had been blown out. She had seen it. She knew she would never be able to *un*-see it. His brains were all over his jacket. He couldn't possibly have got up again.

The figure was now out of sight and not yet showing up on any of the other feeds as they flicked from location to location every few seconds. Shania shook her head and then gathered up the wood. She couldn't think about this. It didn't help. Whatever was happening outside this room, she had to block it out and carry on with her plan.

She carried the paper and the wood up the little stairwell onto the school roof. Walking quietly to the centre, still carefully avoiding the perimeter in case she was spotted, she knelt down in the shelter of the old brick chimney and stacked the splintered wood into a small pile. She stuffed screwed up bits of paper into the gap underneath the wood and then got out her lighter. Flicking it a few times with shaking hands, she then got a steady flame which she put to the paper. The paper caught quickly, writhing and blackening under the flame's blue caress. It smelt sweet and nutty. The wood was not so easy. It sooted over but didn't catch and soon the paper was just ashes. Shania cursed and turned to the bin for more. Then she had a rethink and put the wood into the bin on top of the paper left in it. The bin was metal... it might act like a barbecue. She thrust the lighter down amid the paper and saw it take again. Soon the smaller splinters of wood were smoking. Yes! Now, if the wood lit up properly the flames would get taller... and maybe she could get more stuff to burn... make it big. Make it *noticeable!*

The crackling of the flames must have messed up her hearing. She was so stupidly excited about her little Girl Scout adventure that she didn't even look around until he was right there behind her. The barrel gleamed in the firelight as he took aim.

And he did not miss.

Taking a stand

When the door opened Elliot roared. And the heavily weighted metal stand which he had been swinging to and fro in the darkness seemed to fly up of its own accord in a brutal strike. There was a crunch and a cry of pain and the torchlight spun upwards as the man in black tipped over.

Elliot stood for a second, barely able to believe that he had done it. Then the metal stand and weight crashed back like a pendulum and almost broke his shinbone. The gun! The gun! Where was it? He needed to get the gun. But it was too dark to see; the man's torch was now rolling across the floor, bathing the far wall in odd whirling balls of light.

And it was too late anyway, because David was already back on his feet, cursing and shouting into his radio. Elliot did the only thing he could; he ran. His bare feet seemed to hardly connect with the floor, he went so fast. The drawstring kit bag thumped up and down painfully on his shoulders as his arms pistoned back and forth. He was through the doors and along the corridor in seconds but David was already chasing him; the torch was back in play and as soon as it found him, bullets would follow.

Elliot reached the junction with the main corridor and cannoned straight on through the double doors to the dining hall and the kitchens beyond. Seconds later he slammed into the metal panelled kitchen doors but they did not budge. They were locked. Where now? A right, down the side passage, into the school assembly hall. Up on to the stage. Behind the thick black curtains. Here he stopped for a second, panting hard but trying to be still. Where was David? How badly was he injured? It had sounded like the tennis net stand had broken the man's jaw.

Around him, silence folded in thickly. He could smell the singed dust on the stage lights and the fresh paint on the scenery for the school show. They were doing Grease. Someone had said Shania should audition for Rizzo. Apparently she could sing. Who knew? None of them. Shania had said she'd rather pick gum off the playground with her teeth than be in a stupid school show.

Was that movement? He heard a door thud. Quietly. Someone was in the hall now. *What's the plan, Elliot?* he asked himself. *What now?* He looked around, trying to make out shapes in the gloom of the backstage area. There was a door somewhere, leading to the dressing rooms. Would he be able to get out of a window from there? He really didn't know. He'd never been in the dressing rooms. He wasn't a stage show kind of kid.

He began to move slowly around, shuffling his feet, careful not to kick or knock anything which might make a noise. Beyond the curtains he heard a two-way radio crackle. 'If he's in here it's a dead end,' said someone. He sounded different to David. Maybe this was Abel... or Goliath... or Judas or Noah or bloody John the Baptist for all he knew. What did it matter? It was the enemy. 'Yeah. Get here.'

Something cold struck his shoulder. Elliot caught his breath and felt around. It was a steeply angled hand-rail, attached to a set of metal rungs. He remembered now, that there was a high walkway so the stage crew could access the different spotlights, shift their positions and change the bulbs and coloured gels. He felt out the paddle-shaped rungs and climbed up. The treads clicked and rang under his weight and he prayed it could not be heard beyond the thick stage curtains.

And as it happened, it couldn't - because there was another noise masking it. A sudden thrumming and whirring. With this noise came a sudden shaft of light – a steadily expanding column across the stage, probing its pale fingers through the backstage area beyond. Someone was opening the curtains; using the electric switch which motored them apart. Then came an even brighter light - dazzling him. It was only one skinny strip of the fluorescents which lit the assembly hall. Dim enough normally but right now, like a blinding halogen to Elliot's dark adjusted pupils.

He tucked himself down on the thin catwalk above the stage. He was still in shadow... just. In the middle of the hall stood one man; he'd pulled the black balaclava up over his fair hair, the way the guy in the pond had. Clearly he too was not concerned about ever being identified.

'Listen,' he said. His voice was calm and slow. 'You've impressed us. You've given us a tough chase - and my colleague's smile will never be quite so perfect again.' He chuckled. 'One point to you, son.'

Two, I think you'll find, thought Elliot, *or haven't you visited the pond yet?*

'It's not your fault; it's just bad luck,' the man went on - the direction of his voice shifting as he prowled around the room, gently and relentlessly searching. 'You were just in the wrong place at the wrong time. But it's over now. I know you're in here and you really can't run anywhere else. Come out and talk to me. There might still be a way you can get out of this. We might be able to come to some... understanding.'

Yeah, because I'm brain dead and really going to fall for that! Elliot shrugged the drawstring kit bag off his shoulders. He rested it softly on the thin steel gantry and drew out a yoga stretch band. He tightly knotted one end and then tested the knot with both hands. It tightened and held. Then he reached into the bag and withdrew a single rock-hard sphere. He could feel the double stitching curving across the smooth leather. He sent a small prayer to the cricket ball. *Be true. Be sure. We might get only one chance.*

'You're a clever lad,' went on the soft voice in the hall. 'We could use someone like you. Train you... what do you say?'

Elliot folded the ball into the yoga band slingshot and then, anchoring the knotted end through one fist, pulled it back as far as he could stretch it. The tension made his whole body tremble and he ordered himself calm. He was loaded; cocked. Now he just needed to aim.

Three seconds later, the black figure moved into view. He was smiling as he shone his torch across the stage, left and right into its shadowy wings. 'Come on out, son,' he said. 'This doesn't have to end badly.'

Oh really? I think it does. Just step a little closer. One more step...

If he let the missile go now, it would only reach the man's chest. It needed to reach his head. *Move! Move!* Elliot begged. The strain of holding the cricket ball, primed and aimed, was making him tremble again. Pain was gnawing viciously through his muscles; his arms and shoulders felt as though they were on fire. But if he let the band slacken even a millimetre, the blow would not be hard enough. Years of slingshot practice with stones and rubber band catapults in the woods had taught him that.

One more step!

The man stepped forward and turned to his left, exposing his right temple like a target.

Elliot let the cricket ball fly. And the man hit the hall floor like a felled tree. Elliot exhaled and then sucked in air. His mouth hung open as he dragged breath in and out, his eyes bulging with astonishment. He'd done it! He'd got another one!

He was shaking so much he could barely organize his limbs in any direction but somehow he shoved the yoga band back into the string bag with the four other cricket balls he'd not even needed. Then, slinging his ammo back over his shoulders, he scrambled back down the steps and ran across the stage. The man on the floor was not even twitching. He lay spreadeagled; his torch slid two or three metres from one hand and the gun maybe half a metre from the other. It looked like another SIG. Now that was going to be useful.

Elliot crept closer. The man's eyes were shut and a pink egg-shaped bump was rising on his right temple. SCORE! He should get the radio off his belt too. And then drag the body under the stage.

He stood over the man. Was he dead? A blow to the head of that velocity *could* kill. Hadn't a cricketer died that way just last year? Had he really killed a man? Maybe the second man this evening; he still didn't know whether Jonah had drowned.

No time to wonder. He needed to get the gun and the radio and (*finish the job? asked some dark part of him*) - and get away. The other guy could be here any second. Elliot went to get the gun.

Then he was thrown through the air and pounded onto the wooden floor so hard he could only believe a car must have hit him; the 4x4 from outside must have driven in and slammed him.

The wind was knocked out of him and he could hear himself making a sound like something punctured and dying. It wasn't a car. It was the man on the floor. From being apparently dead, he had risen up like a human man-trap, snapping his limbs around his prey and flipping him through the air. The man's full body weight had landed on his back as he hit the floor, slamming him into the old scuffed wood, driving his two upper teeth through his lower lip and smashing his nose and brow until he saw stars. The cricket balls in his ammo bag punched into his spine. Then the bag was ripped off him and his arms were ruthlessly pulled back and pinned, the strained slingshot muscles sending out burning spasms of pain. A knee drove into the small of his back.

A cold circle pressed against his skull, just above the nape of his neck and a well-oiled click reverberated through it. 'Got you, you little shit!' growled the man. 'Game over.'

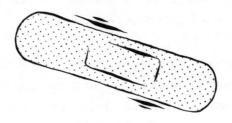

Brains

His aim was true. The life was all sputtered out in moments; a swift end in the half-moonlight of the rooftop. He crouched down next to the remains and let out a long sigh.

Shania made no noise now. It was over. Unrecognisable. This life. All that she had been. All that she had known and thought and believed. Blown away in an instant.

He stared at her glassy eyes and wondered what to do next. What to say.

'Shania. Shania? Can you hear me?'

No response. Pupils wide; dilated.

'Shania. I had to do it. I couldn't let you go on.'

Silence.

'The emergency services - I can't have them here. Your fire would have brought them, It was an excellent idea. You see - I said you were clever. You never believed me, did you?'

Shania stared at the flap of skin that fell away from the side of his skull. She could see the bone gleaming through patches of blood and hair. She gazed at the grey stuff spattered across the right shoulder and sleeve of his tweedy jacket. Behind his looming dark shape, thin spirals of smoke drifted away into nothingness. The gleaming canister of the fire extinguisher lay on its side next to the blackened metal bin, its work done.

'Shania. I think you may be in shock.'

It was only when he reached out towards her that she screamed. For less than a second before he seized her and slammed a hand across her mouth. 'Shhhh! Shhhh! For god's sake, Shania - you have to be quiet!' His hand smelt of soot and blood. She felt another unstoppable shriek coming up through her throat and he seemed to feel it too because he shook her abruptly and then clamped her head against his chest.

'Please be quiet! Please!' he whispered.

Slowly he pulled his hand from across her mouth and she found herself whimpering, like a baby. 'Don't eat my brains. Don't.'

'What? What did you say?' he murmured, his voice remote and baffled beyond the sound of his heart thudding in his chest. Wait.

Thudding? Shania struggled away from him and stared up at his face. His eyes, bloodshot and red, were crinkled with confusion.

'You... you're not... undead?'

He gave her a quizzical look. 'What?! *Undead?* As in... Zombie Teacher?'

She pointed to his jacket where the grey brain matter lay in fluffy tracks across the material. He looked down. He convulsed. And for a second she truly believed this was the point when he realised his brain had been shot out of his head and death was finally catching up with him.

The convulsions continued. He plucked some brain from his jacket and then bent double. With stifled laughter. 'Oh dear god - that is... oh dear god,' he burbled, his shoulders shaking. He held out his hand, the palm open, full of grey matter. 'Feel it!' he said. She recoiled, horrified. *What the hell..?*

He grabbed her hand and pressed the matter into it. It felt dry. Warm, even. Not sticky, cold and jelly-like.

'It's,' he rocked back on his heels, wheezing with laughter, 'It's... cavity wall filling.'

'So...' Shania felt hot and cold and then hot again as relief and exhaustion did battle with intense embarrassment. 'You're not...'

'The Walking Head?' he said, trying to get control of his mirth. 'No! No - I am not. Look.' He pointed to the flap of skin on his skull. 'He missed. The bullet struck the window frame, skimmed the corner of the plasterwork post and spilled some cavity wall filling. The deflected bullet still got me - but it was a glancing blow. Enough to carve a groove through my skull and knock me out for a couple of minutes.'

'Elliot said... he said you attacked that guy... you were eating his brains.' Shania could hear herself and she sounded ridiculous. But...

'Elliot really plays way too much XBox,' said Gallagher. 'Where is he? Have you seen him?'

'About 15 minutes ago. We were both up here and they nearly found us,' said Shania. 'Then he threw my boot across the roof to distract them and then let down the fire escape so they'd think he'd gone down it... and then he ran back downstairs while they were peering over the roof.'

'Clever boy,' he said. 'But he left you up here?'

'No - he made a lot of noise so they'd chase him down.' Shania gulped. He had. He had done that. For her.

Gallagher nodded, understanding. 'And then you thought you'd raise the alarm with a fire.'

'Yes! Why the hell did you stop me?!' she demanded.

'Why the hell did you stop me... sir,' he corrected. Then he laughed again as she stared at him.

'You are *kidding* me.'

'Yes. I am.' Suddenly he was serious. He got up and pulled her to her feet. 'I will get you out of this, Shania - and Elliot too, if...'

'If he's not already dead,' she finished for him.

'He's done well so far. He might have got away.'

'But why not raise the alarm?! Why did you put my fire out? You said it was a good idea!'

'It was an excellent idea but I don't want that kind of help. Trust me - I have some very good reasons. I need to contain this. The outside world cannot know about it - do you understand me?'

Shania did not. She shrugged. 'Whatever. So - what are we going to do?'

'There are four,' he said. 'There were five but I took one out.'

'You... you killed him?'

'I did not kill him,' said Gallagher. 'But he won't wake up for hours. He's bound and gagged in the physics store cupboard. It's locked.'

She looked at him with awe. 'What kind of teacher *are* you?'

'Oh, you know. Just an ordinary head, trying to get by.'

'Ordinary heads don't knock people out and bind and gag them.'

'Ever messed with one on Ofsted inspection day?'

She gaped at him. Her world order was shifting so fast she could barely keep up. One minute she was outrunning masked assassins, then she was setting fire to stuff to *attract* the police, then a zombie was attacking her, then her head teacher turned out to be some kind of action hero. Making cheesy jokes?!

'Come with me,' he said. 'We've got to find Elliot.'

She followed him off the roof, both of them keeping low and far from the edge. 'How do you know there are - were - five? For sure?' she asked as they quietly descended the stairs back to his office.

Pausing by his desk, he pulled out a black object with a stubby aerial. 'Picked up a radio from the man whose brains I didn't stop to eat. Have been listening in.' He turned a dial on the handset and it let out some static hisses and beeps. A voice said: 'If he's in here it's a dead end.'

'I'm heading your way,' came back another voice.

'Yeah. Get here.'

'Leave him to me,' replied the second voice. It sounded slightly slurred... and very angry. 'I want to break his pimply little face first.'

'Teenage stereotyping,' muttered Shania. 'He's not pimply.'

'He's seriously annoyed someone,' observed Gallagher. He was flicking through the security feeds, using the keyboard to control them. Shania hadn't known how to do that.

'So - no change there then,' she said. She peered at the grainy images of the corridors, halls and classrooms as they flicked past.

'Whoa - what's that?' Gallagher paused and enlarged the view of a camera in the school quad. The pond had changed shape. Something long and dark was looming up out of it. Every few seconds it juddered. He screwed up his face, trying to work it out. 'It's the bench,' he said, finally. 'Someone's dragged the bench over the pond and...'

'There's someone *under* that metal grid thing!' gasped Shania. 'Trying to escape. Could that be Elliot?' She felt a coldness inside. 'He could be drowning.'

'If it were Elliot,' said Gallagher, now flicking on through all the other feeds, 'they wouldn't be talking about smashing his face in once they find him. As soon as he was in that pond, his captor would have radioed it in. And then he'd have shot Elliot. No. I think we can say we're down to three men now.' He grinned and shook his head. 'Ah. Here's one - and another is on his way. And the third guy - that's Goliath - is still outside manning the perimeter.'

Shania saw the dimly lit school assembly hall. One man stood in the centre of the room, shining his torch slowly around the stage area.

'What if Elliot is there?' she said. 'There's nowhere else to run. They'll get him.'

'We need to get down there,' said Gallagher. 'First aid box.'

She blinked.

'Pass it over,' said Gallagher, still watching the feeds as he gestured to her to hurry.

She located the white and green box on the wall, unhooked it and carried it over to him. 'Do - do you want me to bandage... that.' She waved her hand in the direction of his gruesome head wound.

'No,' he said, grabbing the first aid box and opening it. 'The bleeding's stopped. It's not a problem.'

'Not a problem,' she echoed, faintly. She could see, in the pale light through the window, that his dark hair was thickly clogged with blood around the wound. 'Does it hurt?'

'Like a bitch,' he said, shocking her with his unteacherly language. 'But it keeps me focused.' He emptied out the first aid box. Plasters, bandages, wipes and sterile swab packets tumbled to the floor. Then he punched right through the back of it to retrieve something hidden. His hand emerged wrapped around a gleaming black gun.

'Glock 17 Gen 4. Standard issue for inner city head teachers,' he said, grinning at her as he checked the clip.

Shania decided he was very probably insane.

'Come on,' he said, glancing at the security feeds once more and seeing no movement beyond the school hall. 'Time to instill some discipline.'

Hostage

Just as he began to black out, Elliot was dragged to his feet. His vision was filled with black splodges and tiny sparkles of light. His attacker had his arms pinned behind him and he was beginning to lose all feeling in them - which was at least better than the searing pain.

Suddenly a face was right in front of him. It was very angry. 'You want a fight, lad?' snarled David. His words were thick and indistinct and Elliot could see why. His jaw was swollen and his teeth were sticky with blood. In fact, there was gap. He may have lost a tooth. Elliot had one second to admire his handiwork with the tennis net stand before his own jaw was smashed by the heavy barrel of David's gun. His lips were already swollen and bleeding from chin-butting the floor. Now he felt as if his face had been cracked in two. He heard his scream distantly. He knew he was losing consciousness as he sagged down in the grip of Cain.

'You want to finish him?' asked Cain. 'We've still got to locate Callaghan.'

'Oh, I want to finish him,' grunted David. 'But he might be the easiest way of getting Callaghan to come to us. He's out there and he's already taken two of us. I can't raise Abel or Jonah. No radio contact. No sign on the monitors.'

Cain swore and let Elliot slump to the floor at his feet. 'You think he'll show up for some kid?'

'He hasn't left the building,' said David. 'That's for two reasons. One - he wants to clean this up as much as we do. Take us all out. Or two - he knows there's a kid to rescue.'

Dimly, Elliot felt glad that they still didn't know for sure about Shania. He'd fought. He'd lost. But at least she might yet escape. It wasn't much but it was something.

David keyed his radio 'Callaghan!' he called. 'I'm guessing you're listening in. So here's a little news broadcast for you. We've got... what's your name?' he kicked Elliot hard in the ribs.

'Spongebob Squarepants,' burbled Elliot, through a mouthful of blood.

He was kicked again. Coughing, he wheezed out: 'Elliot Hickman...'

'We've got young Elliot in the hall,' said David. 'You'd better get here in two minutes or we'll start breaking limbs. Get here fast and we'll let him go. Take your time and I'll paralyse him.'

There was no response on the radio.

'He might not have picked up the two-way,' said Cain.

'Of course he picked up the two-way,' said David. 'Both of them. But he might be switching off in case we track him on the signal.'

'Can we track him on the signal?'

'Not from here. Only from the car and Goliath is patrolling now. Come on. Reception.'

They dragged his limp body between them, back through the dining hall and corridor until they were at reception. Then one of them clicked a button and relayed the message again, this time via the tannoy system. The threat to their captive's arms and legs rang eerily around the empty school, this time calling Callaghan – whom Elliot guess must be the man he knew as Gallagher - to reception.

There was a crackle and then his head teacher's voice cut through the thick silence. 'David. Cain. Goliath. You have my attention.'

Elliot felt his sore face screw up in confusion. Since when did zombies talk like that? They just stumbled about groaning. He'd never heard a zombie talk other than groaning 'Braaaaiiins.' Was it possible that Gallagher had never been undead at all?

'You have 90 seconds,' said David, 'before I put my boot through his thigh bone.'

'So - I walk into reception and you shoot me,' said Gallagher, his voice thin and compressed through the radio but still remarkably cool, thought Elliot. His chest hitched with a small grim chuckle. See what it took to finally decide your head teacher was cool?

'Then you kill my student,' Gallagher's voice went on. 'I don't see an advantage in that.'

'We're men of our word,' said David, trying to sound silky through a mouth that barely worked. 'We have nothing to gain or lose by killing Elliot. He can't identify us. It's too dark and we're masked.' He and Cain reflexively pulled their balaclavas back into place. 'We'll let him go.'

'And shoot me,' Gallagher said. 'Still not hearing much to entice me. How about we trade? I have your men. They're still alive. You can give me the boy, take your men, retreat and try to kill me another day.'

There was a long pause. Then David spoke again: 'We negotiate face to face. There will be no further communication. Be visible inside two minutes or I start breaking young bones.' He snapped the radio off and Cain did the same.

Cain dragged Elliot up again, depositing him on a wheeled office chair and pushing it, and him, around to the front of the reception desk. He wrapped his left arm across Elliot's throat and shoulder, clamping him in place, and pressed his gun to Elliot's right temple. David suddenly grabbed his left leg and hauled it up onto the high reception desk. All set up for breaking. Elliot whimpered. He couldn't stop himself. So much for cricket balls and yoga bands. That was cartoon stuff. All this was horribly, horribly real.

David rested his boot on Elliot's outstretched knee and gave a mean snigger. 'Sixty seconds,' he whispered.' Then he stepped away slightly, hiding himself behind a pillar and training his own weapon on the boy's left temple. Even if Gallagher took a chance and shot Cain, David would react too fast for the head teacher to save one wounded teenager.

There was silence in the corridor. Apart from Elliot's shaky breathing and gulping as he prepared to have his leg broken.

'He's not coming,' said Cain.

'Radios back on,' said David. 'Hold your mic button in. He needs to hear this.'

And he raised his boot.

Pond Life

As soon as the radio message had ended Gallagher grabbed her wrist in his left fist, his right gripping the Glock, and sprinted down the corridor. A few seconds along and he suddenly lurched sideways, against the wall.

'What?! What is it?' breathed Shania.

'Nothing. Just... my brain's a bit battle sore,' he said, running on and pulling her into the stairwell. 'The bullet grazed close to my ear. The impact has messed up my balance.'

They sprinted down the stairs. 'Who are you then?' she asked. 'Gallagher or Callaghan?'

'Strictly speaking, neither,' he said. 'It's complicated.'

'OK... so how are you going to save Elliot?' she puffed out. 'Are you going to shoot them?'

'Maybe,' he said. 'Or maybe you are.'

'Me?!' she squeaked.

'Don't knock it 'til you've tried it.'

He took her to the quad, not the hall. Together they pulled the heavy bench off the metal grid on the pond. It was no longer bucking and heaving. 'He's drowned,' she murmured, but as Gallagher's torchlight slid across the surface of the water there was movement and suddenly a pale face bloomed up out of the water, mouth wide, desperately sucking air.

He wasn't drowned but he was exhausted. Too exhausted to attack them as they pulled the grid up. Gallagher held the gun to the man's head and spoke softly. 'You are getting up now, Jonah. And if you do anything that makes me nervous I will kill you. Do you understand me?'

The man nodded feebly as they dragged his sodden body out of the water. He stood, swaying and dripping, pulling in huge lungfuls of air. His gun must still be in the pond along with his balaclava, thought Shania. His face looked puffy and purple. Shania reckoned he'd been minutes - maybe seconds - away from death.

'Pat him down,' said Gallagher 'Check for weapons on his arms, legs and waistband.'

She did, dismissing her embarrassment. There was a knife attached to his right calf. She took it, along with the clipped band which secured it, and then attached it to her own calf.

'Now what?' she asked. 'Elliot's legs will be broken by now!'

He shook his head. 'Not yet. They don't know I heard them. They'll try again.'

A second later the school tannoy system buzzed into life and the threat to Elliot was repeated. Only now Gallagher was to come to reception. 'You have my attention,' Gallagher told them, on the radio, as he shrugged out of his jacket, still holding the gun to Jonah's soaked head. He handed the jacket to Shania and then took his white shirt and tie off, revealing a taut, well-muscled torso. 'Get his top off and put these on him,' he told her. 'Quickly.'

The man allowed her to yank his saturated black jumper over his head. Then she wrestled the shirt on to the dazed, wet man, while her head teacher continued to bandy words with Elliot's captors. 'Button it,' she said, as tersely as she could. She was shaking and fear kept closing her throat but she was determined that he wouldn't know. With fumbling fingers, the man buttoned up the shirt. Next, Shania got him to put on the head teacher's tweedy jacket.

'You can give me the boy, take your men, retreat and try to kill me another day,' Gallagher was saying.

The man on the other end gave him two minutes to get to reception and then clicked off all communication. The radio was silenced and the tannoy stopped buzzing.

'Take this,' said Gallagher and pulled a smaller gun from his trousers pocket. She stared at it in her palm as he swiftly put on the wet black top she'd just peeled off Jonah.

'I don't know-'

'Yes you do. It's easy. You point it and pull the trigger. Safety catch is off. Pretend it's laser quest. Follow me and stay low.'

They dragged Jonah into the corridor and set off towards reception. As they drew close to the corner which would bring them into view, Gallagher pushed Jonah to the wall and rapidly stuffed something into the man's mouth, one hand still steadily training the gun at his temple. Then he handed a roll of flesh-coloured sticking plaster to Shania and got her to tape it across the man's mouth. She did the job fast, despite her shaking hands, pulling the tape from ear to ear.

'Keep your hands up and walk slowly. Stop when I tap you. One sound,' hissed Gallagher. 'And you're dead. You understand?' The man nodded frantically, breathing hard through his nose.

'You,' he nodded to Shania. 'Under the bench. Aim low. Don't be afraid to shoot if you have to.'

Some distance around the corner they heard someone say 'He's not coming.'

Gallagher pushed Jonah ahead of him and reached the corner just as David said: 'Radio back on. Hold your mic button in. He needs to hear this.' There followed an urgent - pitiful - whimper and Shania held her breath.

'Wait,' said Gallagher. 'I'm here.'

Full Tweed Jacket

Elliot squeezed his eyes shut and waited for the worst pain of his life. Then a voice rang down the corridor. 'Wait. I'm here.'

His eyes sprang open again. The boot was hovering over his outstretched leg. And down the corridor, the dim outline of Mr Gallagher emerged; his hands held high.

'To the last second,' murmured Cain. 'Nice. Waiting for the kid to piss his pants?'

Elliot glanced down to check. No. Not this time. Not yet.

'I can give you back your men,' said Gallagher. 'I know where they are. They're disabled but they're alive. Just send Elliot out of the building. As soon as I see him go through the gates, I'll take you to Jonah and Abel.'

'You'll take us anyway,' said David, easing back behind the pillar and holding the gun. 'Get down on the floor.'

'Let him go,' insisted Gallagher. 'Or your men will be found and interrogated and the trail back to you will be easy. I'm giving you all a chance to get out clean. This has been a total shambles and you know it. But you can all be gone in ten minutes. Live to fight another day.'

There was a long pause. Elliot felt beads of sweat roll down his face.

'You're chancing a lot on my concern for two men who failed me badly tonight,' said David. He peered around the pillar and raised his gun. 'We'll find them. Then I'll probably kill them myself. But first - you.'

And he shot Mr Gallagher in the chest.

The man juddered, thrown backwards, and flopped down on the corridor floor with a muffled shriek.

From her position under the bench, Shania saw him fall and knew she had only seconds left. 'Stay down! Aim!' hissed Gallagher.

This was insane! Did he really expect her to aim and fire a gun when she had never done it before? Except... she had. Not like this. But yes... before. She had a sudden flashback to the day when he'd caught her with a ball bearing gun, in the woods at the back of school. It hadn't been her gun - it had been Aaron Miller's. She'd seen him messing about with it behind the drama block. She'd whipped it out of his idiot hands and run into the woods with it. What kind of retard took a BB gun to school with him? Even she wasn't that stupid.

While Aaron was pounding clumsily through the trees, yelling at her to give it back, she had shot a line of puncture wounds down the trunk of an old oak. Quite a neat line. She was fascinated by the way she had only to squeeze a trigger and a sudden explosion of bark occurred four or five metres away. She was handing it back to Aaron with a crowing laugh when Gallagher had silently emerged from the trees and marched them both up to his office.

She should have been excluded. She'd never worked out why Gallagher was so calm about it. Aaron got a suspension for bringing it to school – but she got just a verbal warning. And a comment that she should take part in target sports. Like *hell*.

Well, she was taking part now, wasn't she? She was about to represent the school in low level marksmanship. She lay on her front, shielded by the bench and several stacks of history text books, and watched the scene unfold.

Jonah was lying on the corridor floor, his arms thrown back and his face turned to her. Above the plaster pinning his mouth shut, his eyes were wide and staring.

Shania became aware of Elliot crying. Sobbing. She did not blame him. He didn't know what she knew.

Footsteps sounded down the corridor, coming closer where the body lay in its dimly glowing white shirt and tweedy jacket. David leaned over and flipped the man's face upward with the barrel of his gun. The second he recognised the taped up features of Jonah, the dark figure crouched in the shadows to his left shot out like a trap door spider and seized him.

The man was caught off guard and barely had time to grunt before he was brought to the floor and his gun wrestled from him. 'Tell him now,' hissed Gallagher. 'Tell him to let the boy leave unharmed. Or *you* are going to be harmed. Very, *very* harmed.'

Through gritted and bloodied teeth, David bawled out: 'Let the boy go! Do it NOW!'

There was a long moment of silence and then Shania heard a scuffling sound. And a door opening and closing. 'He's out,' came back the sullen voice of Cain.

'Radio Goliath. Call him in,' said Gallagher. 'He is NOT to go after Elliot, do you hear me?'

They heard Cain obey with a rapid radio message. 'Come in now. Ignore the trip signal. Come in to reception.' Cain grunted and they heard a crackly affirmative from Goliath.

Gallagher hauled David to his feet and walked him out into the corridor, pressing the gun to his temple.

'Put your weapon on the floor and kick it down the corridor towards me,' he called out to Cain. Shania heard a clunk and a rasp as the weapon spun along the tiles. 'Good,' said Gallagher. 'Now lie face down on the floor with your hands behind your head. Fingers meshed.' There was a faint scuffling sound and Shania assumed Cain had complied. 'Thank you,' said Gallagher. He had never sounded more polite. More calm. And more terrifying. 'Now. It's over. You know it. The only question now is whether I despatch you here and now or call in my team to take you in.'

David gave a small growl of frustration. Then there was movement further along the corridor and it was clear that Goliath had entered the reception area.

'DROP YOUR WEAPON!' yelled Gallagher.

There was a pause and click.

'Tell him to drop it or I will drop you,' Gallagher snarled into David's ear.

David spoke wearily: 'Drop it, Paul.'

'On the floor, face down, hands on head,' said Gallagher.

Shania watched the two men from her hiding place. She took a moment to breathe out and rest her gun on the floor. Maybe she wouldn't be called upon to fire it after all. Gallagher seemed to have it all under control now. Her instructions had been simple. Plan A was to fool the men in the dim light with one of their own dressed as Gallagher - draw one out and then seize him as a hostage. If this looked like going wrong, she was to stay hidden but try to shoot the bad guy in the leg. And hope she didn't hit her head teacher by mistake.

She had not liked the sound of Goliath coming in. Surely it would have been better to handle these two first and then go after Goliath. But she realised that Gallagher had no choice if Elliot was to get away alive. Elliot running outside would trigger this perimeter alarm they'd set up and Goliath would get him unless he had other orders.

'What you need to understand,' said Gallagher, 'is that something much bigger than you is happening here. Your petty vengeance, Forde, is wasting my time. Tracking me down here has put you all in the way of an operation that I cannot shut down. And letting you live to tell tales could be a serious compromise.'

'So end it, then,' snarled David - or 'Forde', as this seemed to be the name Gallagher was using.

'Ah, but I know what all of you are thinking,' said Gallagher. 'I'm alone. Three against one. As soon as I shoot one of you, the others will take their chance. I'm pinned to this position. Your weapons are still on the floor. What have you got to lose?'

There was a thick silence.

'So I will be straight with you,' said Gallagher. 'I don't like killing people. Not even lowlife like you. I only do it if necessary. I'd rather get you taken in. And as it happens, I'm not alone.'

'Christ - the screaming girl!' grunted David.

'Yes, the screaming girl,' said Gallagher. 'Shania - can you step out please?' He sounded as if he was asking her to hand in some homework. She emerged from beneath the bench. 'Is the safety still off?' he added.

'Yes,' she croaked. The small gun was heavy in her sweaty hand. She coughed. She must not sound afraid. 'Yes, it is,' she said in a louder, calmer voice.

'Good. I need you to do something for me. It won't be nice, but I know you can.'

She gulped as David flicked his eyes around to look at her. It was the first time she had actually been seen by one of the gunmen.

'Just understand, Shania, that any one of these men will shoot you or slit your throat the second he gets a chance. Do you understand that?'

'Yes,' she said.

'Good. Now... Shania. Please do as you're told.'

Boundaries

Elliot ran for the trees. The school was surrounded by high metal spike fencing and the gates were locked shut electronically after hours. His student ID would trigger the de-locking of the pedestrian gate but his school ID was in his bag, and his bag was still in his locker. Maybe Gallagher would make the gates open from reception but they were shut right now and he wasn't taking any chances. He'd be a sitting duck, waiting there.

His best hope was to get to cover and hide. Maybe Gallagher didn't know about the guy working the perimeter. Elliot expected to be shot in the back by Goliath at any moment. So he ran and he did not look back. He would rather not see death coming. He'd had too much good luck already; there was no way he would dodge a bullet for a third time.

Then the trees folded around him like a protective cloak. It took him a few seconds to truly *believe* he had made it. In the deep dark he stumbled against a trunk and gripped it tightly, his chest hitching. Warily, he turned and stared back towards the school. He saw nobody chasing him. But he thought he caught a glimmer of glass as the door to reception swung shut.

He was free. Almost. He just needed to get across the fence and get help. Gallagher was still in there - and even though he was obviously *not* a zombie and quite clearly impressively in control, Elliot still didn't fancy his chances. He hadn't forgotten how Cain had pretended to be stunned or dead - and then seized him like an alpha predator. There were still three of them and only one of Gallagher. And what about Shania? Was she still up on the roof?

Elliot turned away from the school and concentrated on moving through the trees without getting his eyes poked out by low branches and twigs. He knew that the perimeter fence ran along the back of this small copse. It was taller than him and the spikes were pretty nasty, but there might be a way over. On the other side of the fence was a row of back gardens. He could see some light chinking through the foliage, the scattered glow cast by people's dining rooms, kitchens and conservatories as they sat down to their evening meal, oblivious to the life and death horror story playing out in the school just a hundred metres away.

He might be able to call for help, through the chain link. Maybe someone would be out in their garden. At this hour on a cold November evening it was unlikely but it was all he had.

He pressed on, becoming aware of his face aching and his swollen mouth stinging. Every limb was sore and complaining - but the relief of escape was immense. Only, it wasn't over yet. He felt like a mouse, allowed to run, while an amused cat stalked it for fun.

He reached the fence, drawn to a part where light was strongest on the other side. The gardens were long and thin but he could clearly see a kitchen window, lit up and golden. It looked like a darkly framed rectangle of heaven. He could even smell dinner - sausages. Mash, maybe. Tears tracked down his face, making his wounds tickle and sting. He needed to shout. He opened his mouth and took a deep breath.

There was a bang. And then another one. Horror-struck, he dropped into a dark knot of ivy. They were coming for him after all.

Seconds passed as he curled into a ball and whimpered unstoppably. He sounded like a disgraced, whining dog. But when nothing else happened he began to understand that the gunshots had been a long way away. Back in the school, in fact. Maybe two people were dead. Maybe those two people were Gallagher and Shania.

Cuckoo Spit

Shania tried to be sick in the waste bin at reception. Nothing much came out. She could hear the men screaming, somewhere beyond her heaving and coughing and as sweat beaded all over her skin and faintness tried to push her to the floor, she felt as though it was *she* who was horribly wounded. Not them.

'Shania. Take deep breaths,' called Gallagher, over the groaning and crying. 'You did really well. Stay with me.'

Shania took a long, deep breath, picked up the dropped torch and slowly stood up. She shone the blue beam of light back down the corridor at the two men. Their faces, as they'd rolled over in agony, were full of pain and also astonishment. Whatever else they had expected when they set out on this evening's murder mission, it wasn't to be shot by a schoolgirl.

Gallagher had told her what to do - and where to aim. 'Around the knee,' he'd said, passing her David's torch.

The men on the floor immediately started shouting out in protest and wriggling around.

'I don't know how good a shot she is,' Gallagher advised, loudly. 'A moving target might get a bullet somewhere else. And I don't just mean the head.'

'I - I...' Shania had wanted to cry. This was too much. But she knew what Gallagher had said was true. Their advantage was too slight. The odds of them *all* getting out of this alive depended on her. Once the men were disabled... 'Couldn't I just tie them up or something?' she'd asked.

'You want to get close to that?' No. No she did not.

She directed the torch, using the beam. The men were still now. Shaking, but still. Logic had won. Better a bullet to the leg than death... or no hope of ever fathering baby assassins. She had aimed and fired.

The scream was awful. She knew she would hear it for the rest of her life. Even so, she had done it again.

Gallagher was standing steady with David still at gunpoint. 'Shania,' he said, in a calm, reassuring tone. 'Don't waste your time feeling bad. Believe it or not, you have just saved those men's lives. If you had not been able to disable them, I would have had to kill David here and then take them out too - and I wouldn't have aimed at the knee.'

Shania nodded, dumbly, watching wet darkness seeping from the men's trouser legs and across the floor. The gun lay in her skirt pocket, hot from firing. The noise it had made was still ringing around her head.

'Listen. Open the desk drawers. You'll find some gaffer tape. Throw it down to me.'

She found it and threw it. Then Gallagher made David tape up his comrades, as he kept the gun steadily levelled at him. The men put up no fight. They were in considerable pain and the grunting and groaning never let up.

'Now you,' said Gallagher, when David had used most of the roll. 'On the floor, face down, hands on the back of your head.' David did as he was told and an eerie kind of calmness settled.

'Shania - you'll want this,' said Gallagher, throwing something shiny towards her. She caught it and stared at it. It looked like something from another world. Another time. It was her phone. 'Switch it on and call this number.'

It wasn't 999. It was another, five figure number. Someone answered it immediately and then she had to repeat a series of code words and co-ordinates, fed to her by Gallagher. It didn't make much sense but apparently it was perfectly clear to the woman on the other end. 'Tell him an extraction team is on the way,' said the woman. 'Sit tight.'

By the time Shania had repeated this, the woman had hung up.

Gallagher nodded and smiled at her as he held the gun in its steady trajectory towards David's head. 'Top marks,' he said. 'It'll be over very soon now. Well done.'

There were a few moments of silence. Then he said: 'Two guns is better than one, by the way.' So she took the gun out of her pocket and trained it on David too.

'Why is this happening?' she asked.

'It doesn't matter,' he said, with a sniff.

'I want to know,' she insisted.

'Oh Shania,' he said. 'How many teachers have longed to hear that?'

'Ha bloody ha. I mean it. Why did they try to kill you? Because... five men... to kill one head teacher. Seriously? What did you do?'

'I put his kid in the bottom set.'

'Jesus.'

'Later, Shania. I will explain later.' Gallagher gave another sniff.

She realised his chin was dark and shining. Flicking the torch across his face she saw a thick river of blood falling from his left nostril.

'Are you alright?'

'I'm fine,' he said. But he didn't look fine. His voice sounded weaker. He was swaying slightly.

'Sir..?'

He lurched suddenly sideways and hit the wall. He was on his feet again, alert, a second later. But a second was all it took. David shot up from the floor and launched at him. One moment there was stillness and a tense calm - and the next the two men were a knot of flailing limbs and blows as David tried to wrestle the gun from Gallagher's grip.

Shania stood, frozen. The taped up men, hands and feel bound behind them, lay on the floor, staring up at the action, eyes alight with hope.

The fight was vicious - back and forth across the corridor in her torchlight. Heads cracked against walls. She screamed and held the gun up. "I'LL SHOOT! I'LL SHOOT YOU! STOP!' But the man paid her no heed - and of course, she couldn't shoot; there was no telling who she would hit. He would know that.

She dropped to her knees and pressed the gun against the head of Cain. 'I'LL SHOOT HIM! I'LL SHOOT YOUR MEN!' she shrieked.

But David didn't even glance her way. He drove his knee upwards into Gallagher's belly and the man doubled over, only to twist around and crack David on his wounded jaw with the Glock. They both went down in a tangle of pistoning fists, knees and feet.

'SHANIA,' yelled Gallagher between blows. 'RUN! GET OUT!'

But she couldn't. Her feet would not carry her to the door. She'd been his back up. She couldn't just leave him. There had to be a way to stop this. She remembered, years ago, there'd been a dog. She was very young at the time but she remembered the dog. A dark cross breed of terrier and Labrador. It was OK but it would turn on you in an instant if you caught it on a bad day. Once it attacked another dog the street and the only thing that would stop it was a high pressure hose. The water stopped the attack.

She stared around. There was a water cooler in reception, but even if she could lift it, she couldn't direct it. If not water - what?! What else? The red fire extinguisher clipped to the wall gleamed at her. Winked at her. She had never even seen it before. Never really thought about such a thing until Gallagher had killed her fire up on the roof. Pocketing the gun, she grabbed the canister and grasped the black nozzle on the top, pulled out the metal pin, and crashed her fist down on the lever. It coughed out a short white jet. It worked.

She ran with it to the fighting men, clamped it under one arm, pointed the nozzle towards their heads, pinched the trigger and blasted. A torrent of thick white foam coated them at breath-taking velocity. She tried to aim it at David but in seconds she had no idea who was who. She just kept pressing and aiming and eventually the adversaries became a writhing white shape, like wrestling snowmen. She heard choking, grunting, coughing. She kept blasting. Then she heard a muffled shot and the white, shuddering heap collapsed.

Shania froze. The frothy jet continued to fly from the nozzle for several seconds before she was able to relax her fingers. As it spattered to a halt there was stillness. A few twitches; nothing more. She put down the fire extinguisher and picked up the torch. As soon as she shone it on the white foam she saw the crimson flower blooming out from the cocoon.

A shadow fell behind her. She spun around, pulling the gun out of her pocket.

'DON'T!' It was Elliot. Hands up. He'd come back.

'I heard shots,' he said in a voice not much above a whisper as he took in the scene around him: two bleeding men bound in gaffer tape, his classmate pointing a gun at him, and a thick indoor snowdrift.

She lowered the gun. 'So why the hell did you come back, idiot?' she breathed.

'I couldn't just leave you here,' he muttered. 'And... I couldn't get over the fence anyway. Where's Gallagher? And the other guy?'

'They're in there.' She pointed to the mass of white foam. They both stared at it for several seconds. Then Shania said: 'Did you ever find cuckoo spit on bushes?'

'What?' He screwed up his face, at a loss.

'That stuff you see on bushes - on leaves - in the spring,' she said, her voice thin and flaky. 'Like someone spat on it. Cuckoo spit, they call it. It's got a little green bug hiding inside. A nymph.'

'A nymph?' Elliot echoed.

'A froghopper nymph. I found one. I opened up the spit with my finger and looked. I found this green bug. I looked it up.'

'You? You looked something up?'

She gave him a hard look and put the gun back in her pocket. 'They're both hiding in there,' she said, pointing at the white mass. 'But I don't know if they're dead or alive.' She started to cry. 'I have to open up the spit and look.'

Elliot took her hand. It wasn't the weirdest thing he'd done this evening. '*We* have to look,' he corrected. 'Come on.'

They scooped away the white froth with their hands. Both men were slumped and still. The shining face of David emerged first. There was a snow-white foam frosting across his eye sockets. When Elliot thumbed it away he found the eyes were open. He grabbed the man's lifeless shoulders and pulled him off the body beneath. A trail of dark pink foam followed.

Gallagher lay on his back. They excavated him carefully. His eyes were closed and there was more bloody foam around his mouth. Shania smoothed it away. She stared at the man's still face and tried to hold the sob inside her. She knew if she let it out, hundreds, thousands more would follow. She would sob for days. Had she done this? Had she suffocated him?

Then a small spurt of froth erupted. Two blow holes appeared from his nose. Froth-lined eyes opened groggily.

'He's alive!' cried Elliot.

'ON THE FLOOR! NOW! HANDS ON THE BACK OF YOUR HEAD!'

Official Secrets

'Tea,' said the woman. 'Drink it.'

Elliot clasped the polystyrene cup with both hands, hoping he wouldn't shake the hot liquid all over his knees. He managed to get it to his lips. It was very sweet.

'Extra sugar,' said the woman, noting his wince. 'It helps with the shock.'

'What *is* this?' muttered Shania. 'Eastenders? A cup of rosy lea supposed to make everything all better, is it?'

'Where are the emergency services?' asked Elliot.

'We're here,' said the woman. She didn't look much like a paramedic. She was dressed in black, much like their attackers. Her face, in the light of some battery powered lanterns they'd set up in the corridor, was smooth and oval, beneath a pony-tail of auburn hair. When she smiled she was very pretty. But she didn't smile often and who could blame her? It was her job to 'sort everything out'. This is what she had told them after they'd been flung to the floor, pinned, patted down and finally released as Gallagher came out of his state of semi-consciousness and took control.

At least a dozen people seemed to be running around the school now, collecting the gunmen - two dead, three alive - and gathering evidence. Or... maybe not. Because from where he was sitting it looked very much like they were *cleaning up* evidence. They hadn't put the lights on; they were just using those lanterns which spilled a cold grey gleam on everything. If he didn't know better he would think they wanted to keep everything dark.

'You're not really the emergency services, are you?' he asked the woman.

'Oh, we are,' she insisted, dropping a blanket around Shania's shoulders. 'Just not the regular guys. Don't worry. We'll have you home safe and sound very soon.'

'You're a clean up crew, aren't you?' he said. She ignored him and sent in a young man, similarly dressed, who brought a large medical case and started attending to the damage on his face.

'Is Gallagher alright?' asked Shania. 'Because, like, I nearly suffocated him.'

'He'll be fine,' said the young man.

'He was bleeding. His head was shot! He was losing his balance!' snapped Shania.

'He'll be fine,' repeated the young man. 'And so will you,' he said to Elliot, as he applied something very cool and stinging to his face. 'This should take the swelling down quickly. You can go home looking more or less normal. Just say you've been in a fight.'

'What?' said Elliot. 'You want me to make up a story?'

'Yes,' said a voice behind him and they all spun around to see Gallagher. His head was neatly bandaged and the blood had been cleaned away. He looked tired, but alert.

'Sir... what is all this?' asked Elliot.

'What it is, Elliot, is classified. Top secret. Do you understand what I'm saying?'

Shania rubbed her face. 'Like... Mission Impossible?'

Gallagher smiled and then winced and put his hand to his head wound. 'Yes - Mission Impossible. If you like. I'm going to tell you what's been going on - not just tonight but for the past four months - and then you should understand why you will have to make up a story for your families. Or, in your case, Shania, the staff at the home.' He looked at his watch and said: 'It's ten past nine. Please tell me you've both stayed out this late before. I'm counting on your bad behaviour.'

They shrugged and nodded. Yeah. Plenty of times.

He handed Elliot his phone, liberated from the school cabinet. 'Both of you - text home now and say you'll be back soon. With all the usual attitude, please.

There was a message from Elliot's mum. **Where RU? Dinner in oven. Gone out with Dave**. It had been sent at 7.15pm. Elliot stared at it in a state of appalled wonder. He'd been fighting for his life since 5pm - and he still hadn't even been missed.

Shania had three texts from the duty house parent. She showed them to Elliot and Gallagher:

Got a text from school to say you're in detention. Please come straight back after.

Then: **Do NOT go into town. Come back. We need a discussion**.

And then, at around 7pm: **Text back or your allowance will be docked by half**.

Gallagher nodded. 'Good,' he said. 'Bad luck about the allowance.' Shania gaped at him as he took her phone and Elliot's and showed their text messages to red-ponytail woman.

'See,' he said. 'We're good.'

'Hmmm,' she said, glancing at them both. 'They do seem to have come through it pretty well - but they could fall apart tomorrow. It's risky.'

Gallagher stood next to her and looked at them both too. He folded his arms. 'I know them well. They're trouble. He's a chronic underachiever because he's got father abandonment issues and spends too much energy trying to be tough. She's an attention seeker and a rebel - classic care home kid. Rejected and emotionally neglected.'

Elliot and Shania gaped at him and then at each other. No adult had ever said anything quite so brutal to them in their lives before. The head teacher seemed to have absolutely no problem with summing them up in a few heartless sentences.

'They're both very intelligent,' said Gallagher and now Elliot and Shania's jaws, only just ratcheted up, dropped even further. 'Bottom sets academically, of course, but both with full street smarts, sharp as a tack and - as we've seen tonight - remarkably resourceful. Brave. Team players - they looked out for each other. And most important of all, they're very, *very*, unlikely.'

'They'll have to sign,' said the woman.

'Of course.'

'Sign what?' snapped Shania. 'I'm not signing anything!'

'I'll get them faxed through,' said the woman, with a sigh. 'Are you sure about this?'

'Definitely,' said Gallagher and she stalked away up the corridor towards reception. Through the low glass window beyond the desk, Elliot could see the wounded men being stretchered into an ambulance. A black ambulance. With no flashing blue lights and definitely no siren.

'So – this is all being hushed up,' he said to Gallagher as their head teacher sat down on the bench next to him. 'Are you going to tell us why?'

'Yes – but after I've told you, you will have to sign a pledge to never speak of what's happened here. Official Secrets Act.'

Shania spluttered through her tea. 'You're kidding!'

'I'm not. Shut up and listen. I am a qualified teacher – I qualified many years ago – but this is actually my first job in a school. I was recruited by the government eleven years ago, while I was finishing my teaching degree, and I've worked as a special operative ever since.'

He paused and they stared at him, genuinely speechless. He went on: 'I've worked on many operations around the UK and abroad over the years, looking after the British people. The reason I came to your school this term was not a sudden change of career. I am in what is known as 'deep cover'. I'm not here to knock your rather poor school into shape – although I've been giving it a go – I'm here to look after a specific student.'

'Who?' they said, in unison.

'He's not here yet. He arrives in January.'

Elliot dug his fingers into his hair. His head hurt. He felt as if he'd been playing Dark Assassin or Black Hawk Ops for 12 hours straight – bug eyed and brain-drained. 'So... what's so special about this kid?' he asked.

'I can't tell you that yet,' said Gallagher. 'But there are very good reasons for the boy to come here. A huge amount of effort has been put in here at Oakwood Academy, in preparation, and it's incredibly important that nothing disrupts it. The whole operation would fall apart if what happened here this evening gets out. Do you understand what I'm saying?'

'Erm... if you didn't want disruption, what do you call all *this*?' asked Elliot. 'Hasn't it all been blown out of the water? And what *did* happen here tonight?'

'Samuel Forde – the man you heard referring to himself as 'David' was coming after me because of a completely different matter. I ruined some arms smuggling concerns he had. And I killed his brother. Tonight was a vengeance thing.'

Shania shook her head. 'Where did reality go..?' she murmured.

'Forde runs a very tight, small unit - most of them ex-Army - and we're pretty sure the five men here tonight are as far as it goes. One of them is already talking to us though, trying for a deal. It seems Forde spotted my photo by pure chance. On a Local Education Authority website, for god's sake! Tracked me down and travelled up from London to pick me off, dump my body in the Thames and make a big statement. They like to make statements, these small time gangsters. Anyway - we'll investigate of course, but assuming we can keep a lid on all this, we may still be able carry on with the operation here at Oakwood.'

'Two men dead and three injured,' said Elliot. 'How do you keep a lid on that?'

Gallagher smiled tightly. 'Trust me. We have ways. You don't need to think about it. All I want from you is a promise that you will say nothing of what happened tonight to anybody.'

Shania tilted her head to one side. Her spiked up hair was drooping and black mascara trailed down one cheek. 'So... it's our little secret is it?' she said. She rolled her eyes. Elliot could see she was layering on the attitude with a trowel because just beneath it she was exhausted and freaked out. He wondered if anyone ever gave her a hug. It would be like embracing a spiny crab.

'No, Shania. It's not 'our little secret' – it's 'our bloody HUGE secret' and if you don't keep it there will be consequences.' There was a chill in Gallagher's voice.

Shania shivered. She pulled the blanket tighter around her. 'Fine,' she muttered. 'I'm not a snitch, anyway.'

'This I know,' said Gallagher. 'But actually I want more from both of you than your silence. I want you to come through tonight and recover. And then I want your help.'

Shania blinked. 'Seriously? Us?'

'Yes, you. I already have some inside help among the staff. Two of my team have been in school for several months too. But I can think of nothing... cleverer... than having two students on the team too. You would be an additional level of security and surveillance. You'd be trained. And you would have to be absolutely silent about everything that is happening. Your family, your social workers – none of them could know. You'd probably have to lie. Would you find that difficult?'

Shania and Elliot looked at each other and then back at Gallagher, shaking their heads. No. They would not.

'Good,' said Gallagher, as the woman returned with two warm sheets of paper, fresh from the school fax machine. 'Sign here.'

For Britain

'Shania! Did you hear a word I just said?' Mr Fawkes was on his feet, prowling the classroom. His face was red and sweaty, as usual.

Shania blinked. She had barely slept last night. She'd got an earful from the duty house parent after she said she'd gone into town. Finally she'd gone to bed, too tired to even eat anything. But as exhausted as she was, her mind and her nervous system had just refused to calm down. In the end she probably got a few fractured hours between 3am and 7am when it was time to get up again. Now she was starting to drift off.

'Shania! Are you listening to me?!'

'Honestly, sir?' she said, leaning back in her chair. 'Not really. I'm a bit sleepy.'

'Let me guess,' he sneered. 'Up on Facebook all night?'

Shania widened her eyes. 'You're *so* down with the kids, Mr Fawkes.'

He stopped by her desk and pounded a stubby finger on her blank exercise book. 'I want at least a full page on the causes of the Cold War before the end of this lesson, Shania, or there *will* be detention.'

Shania grinned and picked up her pen. Hysterical laughter was pounding up through her ribcage and heading for her throat. She glanced at Elliot who was staring at his own blank page, his bruised chin resting on one palm, looking as spaced out as she felt. As soon as Fawkes turned around she pulled the chewing gum out of her cheek and threw it. It landed on Elliot's desk like a tiny pink jellyfish and he immediately shot her a dark look. Then he saw her face and bit his still swollen lips together. His shoulders hitched.

The giggling could not be halted. It grew and grew and soon the rest of the class were staring at Shania Laker and Elliot Hickman as they convulsed in their seats.

'All right, you two! That's enough!' shouted Mr Fawkes, his face getting quite purple, but they couldn't stop.

'I'm sending you to the head,' he shouted, seconds later. 'So you can explain to him what this nonsense is all about.'

'Can you believe last night?' said Elliot, as they walked along the empty corridor.

'Shush,' she said. Then the giggles took them again and it was as if all the crying they needed to do had converted into a different kind of hysteria. The shattered window in the detention class was already replaced. So was the one upstairs which had taken a ricocheted bullet. The school floors were spotlessly clean. The broken ceiling was as good as new. Better, because it didn't even look new.

'We need to behave,' choked Shania.

'No,' said Elliot. 'Remember what they told us. We need to be exactly like we were yesterday.' He glanced out into the quad where the school caretaker was screwing down the metal grid across the pond. Nobody had asked him about his war wounds. Mum hadn't got home until he was in bed and she and Dave weren't up for breakfast. 'We're trouble,' he said. 'Losers. Same as ever.' He looked at Shania and the way she looked back at him spoke volumes. They would never be the same as ever. Never again.

Elliott kicked a dent in one of the metal lockers. His heart wasn't really in it but, hey, he had a promise to keep.

'OoOOoooh – get you!' sniggered Shania. 'Well done.'

'From now on,' Elliot said. 'We don't misbehave for a laugh.' He rested his hand over his heart. 'We misbehave for Britain.'

The head teacher's secretary sent them through to him with barely a glance. She was watering her plant on a new table, which looked almost identical to the old one.

Gallagher was at his desk, wearing another tweedy jacket, tapping away at his laptop. His head wound was still bandaged but otherwise he looked completely normal. The first aid box was mended and back on the wall.

'Shut the door,' he said. 'Sit down.' They did so, on two chairs set out opposite him. As if he'd known they were coming. 'What have you been up to?'

'Nothing,' said Shania. 'Just having a laugh.'

'Good,' he said. 'I was going to send for you anyway.'

He looked up at them for the first time, his dark blue eyes scanning them intently. He smiled and snapped his laptop shut. 'I wanted to tell you myself.'

What? thought Elliot. *That they were getting some kind of medal? Nah. You didn't get medals for top secret stuff, did you? It would kind of blow the cover.*

'Tell us what?' said Shania, rolling her eyes. She didn't appreciate Gallagher stringing it out like an X Factor judge.

'You're both excluded.'

There was a stunned silence.

'What?!' demanded Shania. 'Are you taking the-'

'Put a sock in it, Shania,' said Gallagher. 'You're being excluded because I need you to go. This isn't working out for me.'

'You can't do that!' squawked Elliot. He jabbed a finger at Shania. 'She saved your life!'

'She did. And you saved hers. And she saved yours – and I saved you both. Can we move on?'

Elliot and Shania lapsed back into stunned silence.

'You will be excluded from Oakwood for the rest of this term,' said Gallagher. 'And then the local authority will find you a new place at Jeffery Academy.'

'But that's miles away,' said Elliot, shaking his head.

'Between now and the new year, you will both receive training in basic self-defence, surveillance and weapons handling,' said Gallagher. 'And when I join you as the new head of Jeffery Academy, we will be working as a team.'

Shania's eyes were like saucers. 'Do we... do we have any choice?'

Gallagher regarded her for a few seconds. 'Do you *want* a choice? I *can* leave you both behind. You can go right back to failure and dropping out if you really want.'

Again, the silence and Shania found she was looking at Elliot.

Wondering what he would say.

Eventually, he raised his eyes to hers. They said nothing but they didn't need to. He didn't want to go back to how it was this time yesterday. Nor did she.

'OK,' said Elliot. 'And I suppose we'll have to keep our heads down and work hard will we?'

'Hell, no,' said Gallagher. 'Just carry on as normal, both of you. It's a great cover. Whenever I send for you everyone will just assume you've been up to no good as usual. Just don't do anything that forces me exclude you. That would be unhelpful. Now – go home. Collect your exclusion letters from Mrs Clarke on the way out. We'll be in touch...'

Minutes later they were outside the school on the pavement. It was beginning to rain.

'Well,' said Elliot, 'I'm not sorry to be leaving this dump.'

'Me neither,' said Shania. She jumped high into the air and shouted a string of expletives at the closing electronic gates, accompanied by some equally filthy gestures.

'See you in training, then,' said Elliot.

'Not if I see you first, loser.' She gave him her usual belligerent stare. Then she smirked as she turned away. 'Don't expect me to be friendly,' she said. 'That wouldn't be normal, would it?'

He grinned at her retreating back and her stupid stuck up hair and her ridiculous shiny Doc Marten's on the end of her skinny black-socked legs.

'Yeah, get out of my face, Laker!' he yelled, sticking two fingers up. He walked off in the opposite direction, back home to Mum and Dave and the beating he was probably going to get when his stepdad found out he'd been chucked out of school.

And he felt better than he had in years.

A taster of Murder by Maths...

Louise Duvall glared at Shania. While everyone else in the room was bending over their work and translating basic French words into English, Shania was running her fingers through her white blonde hair, tufting it up with great concentration. The girl seemed to be going for the recently electrocuted look.

'Shania,' said Miss Duvall, sharply. 'Your hair-do can wait until break. Get on with your exercise.'

Shania held up her hands. They were glistening. 'Sorry, Miss,' she said, chewing hard on her gum. 'I can't pick up the pencil; my fingers are all slippery.'

'With *what?*' The teacher screwed up her face.

'It's wax,' said Shania, holding up a little blue plastic tub. 'Stone Wax. Costs eight quid. Sets your hair like rock. Have you got any tissue, Miss?'

Louise Duvall twitched. She was actually looking *forward* to the end of the lesson now. It would be a relief. She needed to de-stress. She snatched a tissue from the box on her desk and walked down to the wannabe punk star. 'Why are you applying hair products in my class, Shania?' she said, in a low, warning voice. 'How does this help you learn French?'

Shania opened her black-lined blue eyes wide and stared away up to her left for a few moment and then, with a triumphant smirk, said: 'Je suis rayer mon cheval.'

Louise had to press her lips together hard and breathe out slowly. 'Impressive,' she said, eventually. 'So what's that in English?'

'I'm doing my hair!' Shania grinned and held up one waxy hand in a high five offer which her teacher ignored.

'Close,' said Louise. 'But I think you meant to say 'Je suis styling mes cheveux.'

Shania rumpled her brow. 'That's what I DID say. More or less.'

'No. You said "I am scratching my horse". More or less.'

One desk behind, Elliot Hickman let out a snort of laughter. 'Yeah – she loves horse scratching, that Shania. She got banned from Ascot, she did.' There were sniggers all around the room.

Shania twisted round and flung her hair-waxy tissue in his face. He threw his exercise book back at her. There was shouting. The end of the lesson was just seconds away. The bell rang. 'BOTH OF YOU!' yelled Louise. 'STAY BEHIND!'

continued...

They waited, slouched at their desks, sullen and disrespectful until everyone else had filed out and Louise had pulled down the blinds and locked the door.

Then she turned around. They were both on their feet. She took a deep breath and raised her hands. She smiled and tilted her face to one side. She let just one finger give a little beckon.

Elliot came for her first. She ducked his right arm throw and pitched him over her shoulder, depositing him hard on the floor.

Shania lost no chance to attack the moment she was distracted. She tried a foot sweep, hooking a Doc Marten around her teacher's ankle and tugging her left leg out from under her.

Louise twisted in mid fall and took the girl down with her, crushing her to the floor, flipping her and pinning her skinny arms behind her back. Shania launched the back of her head up and almost nutted her teacher on the chin.

Louise bounced up and blocked several more blows from Elliot and then very nearly broke his arm in a half Nelson which left his face crushed against the wall. He let out some suspension-worthy language. Behind them, Shania was on the floor, whining about her wrist being broken.

'Enough,' said Miss Duvall. 'You're both improving. But we need more time on the gym mats. I'm going to break someone's face on a desk sooner or later and that will be a pain. I want you both back here after school – five o'clock on the dot. Don't be late.'

Shania and Elliot stood, rubbing their bruises. 'You don't have to be so... vicious!' said Shania.
'Yeah,' said Elliot. 'We're still learning, you know!'

Miss Duvall smiled, stretched and cracked her knuckles. 'You're coming on,' she acknowledged. 'Now learn some bloody French, the pair of you, and I won't want to hurt you quite so bad...'

About the Author

Ali Sparkes has published more than forty books
for children and young adults.

Starting out as a local newspaper reporter, she went on to
become a broadcast journalist with regional BBC before writing
comedy for BBC Radio 4 and eventually turning to writing books.

She was rubbish at reading and writing in her early school years and
never got an A in any exam she ever took. Didn't go to uni, either.

Who knew, eh?

Also by Ali Sparkes

The Shapeshifter series:
Finding the Fox
Running the Risk
Going to Ground
Dowsing the Dead
Stirring The Storm

The Unleashed series:
A Life and Death Job
Mind Over Matter
Trick or Truth
Speak Evil
The Burning Beach

The Shapeshifter: Feather and Fang

Frozen In Time
Dark Summer
Wishful Thinking
Out of this World
Destination Earth
Car-Jacked
Thunderstruck

Night Speakers

www.alisparkes.com

ALi SPARKES

www.alisparkes.com